OCCAM'S MURDER

A C. J. Whitmore Mystery

by

J. T. Toman

Copyright 2016 by J. T. Toman

For information, email Cozy Cat Press, cozycatpress@aol.com or visit our website at: www.cozycatpress.com

COZY CAT
PRESS

ISBN: 978-1-939816-86-3
Printed in the United States of America

Cover design by Paula Ellenberger
www.paulaellenberger.com

10 9 8 7 6 5 4 3 2 1

Acknowledgements

Thanks to Patricia Rockwell and the Cozy Cat Authors.

For Don, Bryce, and Shana.

TABLE OF CONTENTS

NINE O'CLOCK

9:03 a.m.

James Brimmage loved women. The plump dames were a delicious handful and the skinny gals geometric masterpieces. Even tall ladies posed an occasional, and enjoyable, gymnastic challenge. He rarely said no to a keen one and considered feisty women like jalapenos. Great with tequila, perfect for some extra spice, but not for the every day. Of course, the feministas could be a drag. Always harping on about equal pay, voting rights, and glass ceilings. *Not really an aphrodisiac, ladies.*

James, an economics professor at the renowned Eaton University, considered his attitude towards women consistent with his general life philosophy— "enjoy life now." It was this philosophy that had filled his garage with a Ducati 1199 Panigale motorcycle, the latest in snow mobiles, and his Porsche 911 Turbo. *It's a good thing I'm not the finance professor,* he often thought ruefully. His credit was a mess, and he had huge debts that he guessed he would pay, someday.

Luckily for James, his desire to enjoy the opposite sex was frequently reciprocated and would've been even *sans* Porsche. He was Australian by birth and looked like a model for a Billabong catalog. The man sported bleached blond hair and a permanent tan, courtesy of the Golden Booty tanning salon. Eaton University, a juxtaposition of gothic architectural beauty and modern industrial poverty, was nestled in the town of Elm Grove, in the heartland of southern

Connecticut. The Golden Booty was considered the place to go in downtown Elm Grove to avoid New England winter white skin. It was very popular with the sorority girls of Eaton, and, therefore, according to his "enjoy life now" philosophy, also with Professor Brimmage.

In winter, James supplemented his well-tanned Australian looks with khaki pants and a long-sleeved surfer's tee. Truth be told, while he may have been born in Australia, it'd been many years since James Brimmage had set foot on his native soil. This small fact, however, did not prevent him from dressing "Australian," affecting a strong Down Under accent, and throwing in the occasional "g'day" and "mate" when he remembered. Experience had taught him that all women, or at least a decent majority, couldn't resist an Aussie.

At just after nine o'clock in the morning on the first Monday of the spring semester, James Brimmage was sitting in his office. It was too early in the day for work. Instead, he was relaxing in his high-backed, leather office chair, resting his feet on his desk, and reliving the events of the night before in his mind. An Elm Grove beauty had been appropriately overwhelmed by his Australian charms. He rated her an eight, maybe even an eight-point-five, out of ten.

James was contemplating the wisdom of the morning-after phone call. Sometimes, it was best just to let the memory of the night together serve as the goodbye. James stared out his office window. It was January and the snow was falling steadily. *It's really too snowy to call*, he thought. A call would lead to a date, and he didn't feel like driving out of his way in this weather. He couldn't ride the Ducati, and he didn't have snow tires on the Porsche. So, definitely, no call.

God, what if she calls me? he thought a few seconds

later. *She's just the type that would. Maybe I should see her once more, to make sure things are okay between us.*

A knock sounded at the door, effectively ending James's internal phone call debate.

"Come on in, mate," he called out, his accent a passable imitation of the Crocodile Hunter.

C.J. Whitmore entered the room, her magenta skirt swirling around her ankles and her hot pink cowboy boots clacking against the polished wood floors of James's office. Since arriving at Eaton last November, James had repeatedly, and unsuccessfully, tried to seduce the attractive, mid-thirties professor from Texas, tempted by her long blonde hair and even longer legs. He viewed her singular lack of interest in him as a personal challenge.

"Well, if this snow doesn't frost your nostrils, nothing will," said C.J., by way of introduction.

James looked at the peaks of C.J.'s breasts, pushing against her white, spangled cowgirl shirt. *Hmm,* he thought. *I wonder what C.J. is doing tonight. The snow isn't that bad. I could definitely be free.*

C.J. interrupted his musings. "Hello? James? Anyone home?"

James flashed a brilliant smile at C.J. "Sorry, mate. What was it you wanted to talk about?"

C.J. folded her arms across her chest and snorted in exasperation. "I just told you. I was roped into the job of coordinating the seminars this semester. Peter Johansson fed me some hogwash about setting an example and being a good department citizen."

James nodded, although he didn't understand why C.J. was sharing this particular factoid.

"I need you to present a seminar. Okay?"

James's smile faded as his ever-calculating mind processed her request. James, Mr. Make-Me-Happy-

Now, got no personal enjoyment from talking about his research. There was no career benefit to presenting a seminar at a university where he already had a tenure job. And he definitely didn't want feedback from his colleagues about his work. He didn't value their opinions that highly. But, maybe, it'd be his in with C.J.

"No worries, mate. I'll do it," he replied, flashing his toothy smile at her again. "Why don't you and I grab a coffee today at eleven to talk about it?"

"Love to," said C.J. insincerely, "but I'm rather busy. Why don't I just email you the available slots and you pick one?"

James conceded defeat, for this round, as C.J.'s cowboy boots clacked decisively out of his office before he had a chance to reply.

The offices of the Eaton Economics Department were divided among four buildings. The department hub, 40 Knollwood, was a bright red-brick building. It was here that classes were taught, seminars and faculty meetings were held, and the easily distracted administrative assistant watched the happenings on Knollwood Place from her ground-floor office. Forty Knollwood also housed an elite group of professors who viewed the short distance from their offices to their teaching classroom as corollary to the distance between them and God.

The adjoining building, 42 Knollwood, was a somber Gothic structure of gray stone. This edifice housed senior professors who were quite important but not revered enough that they could get office space in 40 Knollwood. It was also home to the micro-economists and statisticians in the department, and the irony of a depressing, gray building for their office space was not lost on many. "Forty-two Knollwood, a.k.a the morgue," C.J. Whitmore was often heard to say.

These two buildings, 40 and 42 Knollwood, were connected in the basement by the Smythe Lounge. The principal function of this room was that it provided a handy way for the faculty on that side of the street to move between the two buildings without having to trouble themselves by experiencing the outdoors. It's secondary purpose was to provide a place for underfunded graduate students to work on problem sets, keep awake by drinking free coffee, and cadge day-old sandwiches and pastries from catered faculty events.

The other two economics buildings, 41 and 43 Knollwood, were located on the opposite side of the street. These building housed the "remainder" of the faculty. The flotsam and jetsam, as it were. Offices here were assigned to professors who received little grant money or public recognition. The ones who were never invited to the White House, to Oslo to receive a Nobel, or to appear on talk shows, pushing their latest book. The faculty in 41 and 43 Knollwood studied subjects deemed inconsequential by their peers, such as economic history or environmental policy, and would therefore have to cross the road to teach a class, attend seminars, or be present at a faculty meeting.

At first, James Brimmage had been rather affronted to find his office in 42 Knollwood. He fancied himself 40 Knollwood material, especially as he assumed all the secretaries would be in that building. However, the spare offices atop 40 Knollwood had recently been reallocated for the Edmund DeBeyer Memorial Foundation, a foundation made possible by the will of a previous professor. A professor who, James's noted with some astonishment, had not only been murdered, but had also killed one of his colleagues. James privately wondered how bad a crime would have to be before Eaton wouldn't take a person's money and name a building after them. In the meantime, he was reconciling himself to his office in 42 Knollwood, especially after he realized that there was only one secretary in 40 Knollwood, and that was Mary Beth.

9:07 a.m.

Mary Beth Sanders had made only one New Year's resolution—to get a massive diamond embedded on her ring finger. You didn't need a Ph.D. in economics to understand that marrying a rich man was the easiest path to happiness. And, if nothing else, it would mean Mary Beth could leave her boring-beyond-belief job as administrative assistant to the nerds. She sighed deeply as she looked at her hands, still free of De Beers' best.

But, she thought as her gaze lingered on her fingers, *I do have a great manicure.* Mary Beth had opted to celebrate the start of the semester by having little black academic mortarboards painted on each nail, a decision made more startling by her choice of fluorescent green as the background color. "Green means go," she'd explained to a baffled C.J. Whitmore earlier that morning, when C.J. had stopped by the front office for a box of white chalk. "It'll inspire the students to graduate."

"Oh," C.J. had said, briefly lost for words. She stared in amazement at the bright green talons in front of her. "I'll make sure to send the pot heads, drama queens, and stupid-as-mud students your way. I'm sure a quick glance at your fingernails will be all it takes for them to learn the linear regression model."

"You are, like, so right," Mary Beth had agreed, thankful she'd taken the time to go to New York City to get her nails done, instead of letting some cut-rate cosmetology student from Elm Grove butcher the job.

After waiting around in the office for almost an hour after her conversation with C.J., drinking her coffee with fingernails at the ready, Mary Beth and her manicure reluctantly turned to the administrative work for the day. On her to-do list was a rather large photocopy job for Lauren Masters, the new junior professor. In the way that an aging housecat welcomes a kitten, Mary Beth had been delighted to see Lauren Masters arrive at Eaton towards the end of the previous semester, hired as a new assistant professor. Not that Lauren was younger than Mary Beth, a fact that Mary Beth was very quick to point out. But somehow late-twenties on a stunningly beautiful professor seemed younger than mid-twenties on a moderately attractive secretary.

Mary Beth had recognized the problem right away. Professor James Brimmage was her current candidate for Mr. Rich Husband. However, a man like James often had difficulty focusing. The long legs and flowing auburn hair of Lauren Masters were not helping Project Diamond.

"The woman is like a McDonald's Extra Value meal," Mary Beth had explained to her best friend, Annabelle. "Everything you want in great quantities. And she's *cheap*." Mary Beth comforted herself with the thought that she was the fine dining alternative, an Applebee's or a TGIF's. A better quality choice. Unfortunately, it was McDonald's that got the millions of visitors a day.

Encouraged by Annabelle, Mary Beth didn't acquiesce to the role of wallflower quietly. Today, in addition to her magnificent nails, she was wearing knee high, black boots with five-inch heels and cheetah fur trim (*imitation of course…put the cheetah, like, before the boots, people*), a purple faux-crocodile-skin miniskirt, and a very tight, bust-revealing, sheer, black shirt. The crocodile skirt had been Annabelle's suggestion. "It'll show Professor Brimmage that you embrace his culture."

Mary Beth had also tortured her long brown hair into glossy, straight submission early that morning. And her skin sparkled, courtesy of her Absolutely Radiant glitter moisturizer. Mary Beth wasn't taking any chances. One glance her way and Professor James Brimmage would understand what could be his.

In the meantime, however, Mary Beth still had the chore of photocopying hundreds of copies for Lauren Masters. *Whatever,* Mary Beth thought, looking with distaste at the paper before her. *Am I, like, her slave or something?* She flipped through the sheets that were marked URGENT. *This doesn't look urgent. What's a syllabus, anyway? I bet I can leave it until next week.* Putting aside the photocopying, Mary Beth turned on her computer, opened her Netflix account, and started watching *Say Yes to the Dress.*

9:11 a.m.

Betsy Williams stood at the front of the lecture hall, looking out at her Introduction to Microeconomics class. The room was relatively quiet and the students appeared to be filling out her get-to-know-you survey while simultaneously checking their texts. Betsy started every semester by gathering information on her students—why they were taking economics, how they felt about online learning tools, and some favorite hobbies. During the semester, she tried to incorporate this information into her lectures. A case study on the economics of football recruiting, for the sports fans. The financial contrast of a box office success to a flop, to illustrate risk versus reward. The use of cell phones as an affordable business tool in developing economies.

The one example she skated over was the economic returns to education. Students were taught that more education translated into higher salaries. However, Betsy was proof of the imperfection of this theory. She was an adjunct faculty member. A job that required a Ph.D. and paid less than a low-level secretary. Most of the faculty thought of Betsy as a useful departmental tool, like the photocopier or the coffee maker. Some, however, were not so kind. It had taken Betsy a moment to realize that Lauren Masters hadn't made a typo when she'd referred to Betsy as the "road scholar" in a recent email. Rather, Lauren's comment had been a reference to the fact that, as an adjunct, Betsy didn't warrant her own office on Knollwood Place. Instead, her car served as her filing cabinet. Every day she schlepped in her notes and teaching tools and drove them back home in the evening. Moreover, her classes were perpetually assigned the most inconvenient and uncomfortable lecture halls. Today she was teaching in the Forestry Department basement, a drafty room whose only redeeming feature was its proximity to Wallaby's coffee shop.

Despite all of this, Betsy enjoyed teaching at Eaton. At the start of every semester, she felt a small thrill as she looked out at the class. She was always hopeful that one of her students would become President of the United States, write the next great American novel, or solve world hunger. However, it wasn't always clear the students shared Betsy's lofty ambitions for themselves. Today, while Betsy contemplated the talent and potential that sat in front of her, the students amused themselves filling out her get-to-know-you survey. One student wrote "pocket money" in response to Betsy's request for a definition of microeconomics.

Another confessed to the hobby of "breathing." And a tech-savvy student, bored with the pencil and paper format of the survey, had started a text entry betting pool among the class, to guess Betsy's weight. The current favorite was 250 pounds—an answer that would have delighted Betsy by being so low.

Until recently, Betsy Williams had never wasted a thought worrying about her weight. What would skinniness achieve that she didn't already have? Betsy enjoyed her work, had a loving husband, her kids still came to visit, and she spent her spare hours spoiling a tidal wave of grandchildren—seventeen at last count. However, a few weeks ago she'd been given an iPad by her oldest son as a Christmas gift. Within hours, Betsy had started on her Google medical degree. Given her size, she could feel her type 2 Diabetes percolating, her blood pressure rising, and constantly worried that she was minutes away from her first stroke. Just that morning, Betsy had calculated her BMI. The number itself hadn't look so bad—it was only double digits and barely topped 50—until her iPad informed her that a BMI over 25 meant she was about to die.

9:14 a.m.

Walter Scovill pulled down his hardback copy of Greene's *Econometric Analysis* (seventh edition, of course), placed it carefully on his desk, and, using a $100 bill, neatly lined up a column of cocaine on the cover of the textbook. He looked at the little pillar of white glory, almost salivating over the thought of his impending high. It was times like this that Walter wondered how he'd survived the days when caffeine had been his only source of energy. He'd wasted a half-century from sheer ignorance. Not willing to waste even more time, Walter rolled up the Benjamin, bent over, and snorted the line up his nose. He shook his head euphorically. *God, he was great*!

When Eaton University had sent Walter Scovill to the "health farm" last semester, hoping to cure him of his unpleasant personality, the university hadn't considered the unintended consequence of this action. Greg, a fellow "resident" and relapsed drug addict, had been very happy to introduce Walter to the world of the Big-C, a.k.a Candy Cane, a.k.a Snow. Whatever name you called it, cocaine and Walter were now very good friends.

At the present moment, deliciously high and overwhelmed with self-worth, Walter started the day his favorite way—spying out his office window in 42 Knollwood and classifying his department colleagues as either disposable goods (to be used and thrown away, like Walmart t-shirts or teaching assistants), inferior goods (good enough for a cheaper school, like Duke or, heaven forbid, a state school), or poor but passable substitutes for quality (in Walter's opinion, he was the only economist of any value, but it was hard to be a department of one).

Walter leaned towards the window and looked down at Knollwood Place. Charles Covington III, muffled up against the snow, was shuffling towards 41 Knollwood. *Disposable good!* Walter thought emphatically.

But then a glimmer of doubt crept into his mind. It was very hard to hire an economic history professor these days. Econ grad students had become so practical, picking majors that made enough money to cover their substantial tuition outlay. Majors like finance, microeconomics, and econometrics. Walter bet that some state college in the back of beyond would likely hire Charles so they could fill their economic history slot. And they wouldn't blink at the fact he was almost ninety years old. After all, popes and senators seemed to last an eternity. Why not a professor? As a bonus, near-centenarians like Charles could be hired very cheaply, having no concept of the modern value of money. That last fact, at least in Walter's opinion, was the principal reason why Charles was still tolerated at Eaton. Walter reluctantly upgraded his elderly colleague to "inferior good."

Minutes later, Walter noticed Arthur Fleitman walking towards the department, latte in one hand, briefcase in the second. Professor Fleitman sipped at his coffee and didn't seem at all hurried by a desire to avoid the snowy weather. Walter snorted his disgust. During his absence last semester, the department had made several terrible decisions. Like hiring Arthur Fleitman, an antiquated piece of economic yesteryear. *Fleitman is completely disposable,* Walter thought angrily. *A waste of departmental oxygen.* Walter considered himself an expert on Arthur Fleitman, as Arthur had been Walter's Ph.D. supervisor at Princeton. In Walter's mind, Arthur Fleitman was the ghost of economic past, coming back to haunt him.

9:17 a.m.

Had Arthur known Walter's assessment of him at that moment, it wouldn't have changed the nature of their collegial relationship. Walter Scovill was already on Arthur's "things I despise" list. Not that Walter had done anything special to be included. The list of things that Arthur Fleitman despised was very, very long. He couldn't abide any of his former graduate students, he had no tolerance for office politics, and he hated every university administrator he'd ever met. Additionally, he loathed perky coffee baristas and women who wore high heels in the snow like that piece-of-fluff, waste-of-space, junior professor he'd just seen slipping on Knollwood like a fool. And they were just the annoyances that initially came to mind. If you wanted the more extensive list of his dislikes, which ranged from insurance commercials and small children to fitness fanatics and Facebook, he'd be happy to oblige. It would just take some time.

Eaton had persuaded Arthur to leave his long and distinguished career at Princeton with promises of an even larger paycheck, continued tenure, and a glide path to emeritus status. This was another way of saying Arthur Fleitman had come to Eaton with the plan of doing as little work as possible for as much compensation as he could wring out of the college. Arthur knew that Eaton would use his name to impress potential donors. In his opinion, the hefty salary he demanded was simply the market price for his reputation.

When Arthur's former colleagues at Princeton heard the news of his departure, they had held a suitably somber farewell gathering for him before he left and a raucous celebration party after he was gone. Old Art the Fart wasn't going to be mourned for long. As far as New Jersey was concerned, they were welcome to him in Connecticut.

In Arthur's defense, he didn't go out of his way to be curmudgeonly. It was just that he was seventy-six years old and saw no reason that he should be inconvenienced by inconsequential nonsense. A person was allocated a finite number of heartbeats during their lifetime, and Arthur didn't intend to waste any of his on stupidity. This was why he wasn't hurrying to his undergraduate advanced microeconomics class, even though it was snowing and well after the 9:00 a.m. start time. Undergraduate students ranked very high on the list of things that Arthur Fleitman disliked. With their pierced noses, tattoos, and iPhone obsession, Professor Fleitman found them unpleasant to look at, tedious to talk to, and vacuous to teach.

At twenty minutes after nine, Arthur strolled into the basement classroom of 40 Knollwood. He studiously avoided eye contact with the waiting students and didn't waste any energy offering a smile or word of introduction. Instead, with deliberate slowness, he set down his briefcase, placed the remnants of his latte on the lectern, removed his snow-covered trench coat and tartan scarf, and carefully draped both coat and scarf over an empty chair to dry. His setup complete, Arthur Fleitman then turned his back to the class and started writing lecture notes on the blackboard.

The students glanced across the room at each other, eyebrows raised. It was the first day of class and they didn't even know the name of the professor writing on the board before them. The trust funds at Eaton expected better service.

"Excuse me, professor?" a girl in the front row interrupted.

Arthur paused his writing and turned around slowly. "Yes?"

"Well," the girl stumbled slightly under Arthur's unwavering stare. "I was just wondering if you wouldn't mind introducing yourself, and the course, for a few minutes. Um, like, is there a syllabus?"

Arthur considered her momentarily. The girl did nothing to reverse Arthur's dislike of students. He noted an upper-ear piercing and assumed the existence of multiple tattoos beneath her hooded Eaton sweatshirt. "Young lady, ask yourself the following question. 'How much do I want to know my professor's name?'"

The girl looked back at him blankly. "Um," she said, "I did just ask, so I guess quite a bit?"

"Exactly. Rule number one of economics. If something has value, don't give it away for free. If you really want to know my name, the price is $100. The cost of a syllabus is $500. An *A* in the course will set you back five large. Still interested?"

The entire class was now staring at him with wide eyes. This was not the Eaton way. The girl shook her head uncertainly.

"I didn't think so. Now, young lady—and please know that I use that title out of politeness rather than a desire for accuracy—I suggest you worry less about me and concentrate on your own education. You may want to copy down the notes that are on the board before I erase them. Your parents have paid the college quite a tidy sum on the assumption that you'll take advantage of the information offered in this class. And, before you ask, I will be testing today's material on the final."

9:23 a.m.

Walter, feeling the edge of his high beginning to dull, meticulously arranged another line of cocaine and snorted his way back to euphoria. *He was better than great. He was amazing. Stupendous. The best economist that ever lived. Even better than "invisible" Adam Smith or "demanding" John Maynard Keynes.* Chuckling quietly at his economics humor, and eager to amuse himself further, Walter peered back out the window.

Lauren Masters, the new junior hire, was slipping on the snowy street below while texting on her phone. Her patent leather pumps weren't providing much traction in the icy conditions and she was visibly shivering, dressed in a knee-length skirt with only a short jacket over the top. Walter marveled how Peter Johannson had achieved the impossible when he hired her. Somehow, Peter had managed to find the one candidate that was inferior to himself—Peter—in terms of IQ, career prospects, and grasp of fundamental economic concepts. It was even rumored that Lauren Masters had received her Ph.D. from a state college. Walter classified her as a disposable good. *But,* he thought as he watched her long legs stumble towards 43 Knollwood, *one that could be put to good use first.* As a rule, he was only interested in the undergraduate co-eds, but Lauren was worth a second glance.

Walter then caught sight of Peter Johannson arriving for the day. His good humor dissipated immediately. Peter Johansson had been appointed acting department chair during Walter's absence, and there was an election to appoint the permanent chair that afternoon. The department chair was a position of power. The chair controlled the teaching loads of his colleagues; he had access to departmental funds; he had the power to delegate arduous committee work to his least favorite colleagues. In Walter's mind, it was intolerable that anyone other than he, Walter Scovill, would even consider running for chair of the Economics Department at Eaton University. Peter Johannson, however, had no such qualms. He'd decided to run against Walter for the permanent position. In an ideal world, Peter Johannson was a disposable good and Walter would happily dispose of him that morning. *A heart attack would do the job nicely. Or a pack of underfed wolves.* In reality, Peter had become a substitute for Walter, which was troublesome.

Walter needed to be certain he had the votes to win

the election. The problem was that it was the first day of spring semester, a semester known for its cold and snow. This meant the faculty with any brains were still on vacation, having arranged for their teaching assistants to hand out the syllabus. Or even more likely, they'd taken sabbatical for the entire semester, and were looking for research inspiration in Hawaii. He'd have to make sure the simpletons who were around for the vote understood the reality of the situation.

Walter heard the resonating click of C.J. Whitmore's cowboy boots in the hallway outside. *Classic exhibit of a disposable good*, he thought. C.J. wasn't even worthy of a part-time teaching position at an underfunded, asbestos-ridden community college. Now that Walter was back, getting rid of C.J. was high on his list of priorities, and he would start today by making sure he got the chairmanship of the department back.

9:26 a.m.

C.J. Whitmore was noteworthy as the only female in the Economics Department at Eaton University to have ever received tenure. "The first and the last," Walter Scovill whispered under his breath, whenever anyone raised the point. "It's a mistake we're unlikely to repeat."

As department chair, Walter had met C.J. when she'd interviewed at Eaton for the position of junior professor. He hadn't minded her in those early days. C.J. had been appropriately quiet and benign, demurely going along with the boys as she should. It was only after she'd received tenure that problems arose—the outrageous outfits; her vocal opinions; a complete lack of submission. In Walter's opinion, C.J. Whitmore was now a malignant tumor, eating away at the very integrity—the very powerful and masculine integrity—of the department.

Walter's opinion was widespread among his colleagues, though not universally upheld. Some, notably the administrative powers-that-be, felt C.J.'s tenure appointment was a good thing. A token of Eaton's modernization. A sign of the university's coming of age. A sure-fire way to gain fundraising dollars from the co-ed alums.

Others, including a large percentage of the faculty residing in 40 Knollwood, felt they'd been tricked into approving a woman's tenure. How could they have known she was female when she just put her initials on everything? C.J. could just as easily have been Christopher John as...well...as whatever her initials actually stood for. What were they supposed to do? Turn up to job seminars and faculty meetings to actually meet the woman? Please. There was only a finite number of hours in the day.

C.J. was not ignorant of the public opinion that surrounded her appointment. She just didn't waste time worrying about it. After all, the lack of respect felt for her was frequently mutual. As she left James Brimmage's office that morning, arms still crossed over her chest protectively, C.J. wondered if the town of Elm Grove was big enough to contain her fury. *Men!* she thought, outraged. *How about I stare at their crotches all day? Would that be fun? I bet that man's in his office at this very moment scoring me on a ten-point scale.*

The reverberating sound of her boot heels on the wood hallway slowed C.J. down. *Why was she letting this man have the final say? He was, after all, just an over-sexed jackaroo.* C.J. thought for a moment, laughed out loud, and took a few deep breaths to compose herself. She returned to James's office and opened the door without bothering to knock.

"Sorry to disturb you."

"No worries, mate," said James, pleased to see C.J. again so soon. "Do you have time for that coffee after all?"

"Maybe. Could you stand up for a moment so I can decide?"

James, hearing her comment as an assent, swung his legs off the desk and stood up. "Ready when you are."

C.J. gazed intently at James, like a farmer inspecting the livestock. She peered searchingly at his crotch, tilting her head from one side to the other, and pursed her mouth in concentration. Finally, she shook her head.

"I think I'll have to pass on coffee," said C.J., with a smile. "More gelding than stallion, I see. I give you a three out of ten." C.J. paused and stared at James's pants once more. "Lucky for you that grade inflation is so rampant these days." Laughing, she turned and walked out of the room, her arms swinging by her sides.

9:33 a.m.

Lauren Masters adored being one of the few women in a male dominated profession. It lightened her workload immensely. Where some women saw a boy's club limiting their success, Lauren Masters saw testosterone-addled men ready to be manipulated. *Why work for a living when you can flirt for it?*

Lauren always remembered the lament of the only other female student in her graduate school program. "It's so much more difficult for us," the woman had said. "We'll have to work twice as hard to break through the glass ceiling and become full professors."

Lauren had just rolled her eyes. "Glass ceiling, my well-toned ass. You need to turn your thinking upside down."

The woman had stared at Lauren, not understanding.

"Think of it as a glass *floor*. And make sure you wear a lace thong and miniskirt," Lauren explained. "Men will be looking up at you in no time. And you'll be a full professor before you're thirty."

The woman, whose name Lauren hadn't bothered to learn in the five years they were in school together, had just gasped. "You're joking, aren't you, Lauren? Tell me you're joking."

Lauren never joked about her career.

Today, Lauren was wearing black high heels and a Calvin Klein gray wool skirt that ended well above the knees. The matching jacket and sheer blouse were cute, but not noticeably warm. For a brief moment, as she slipped on the snow and ice on Knollwood Place, Lauren had wondered about her glass-floor approach to life. Her legs were freezing and she couldn't even feel her toes. And for what? She'd only seen Charles Covington on her way into work, and Lauren Masters didn't waste her smiles on the powerless.

Cocooned in the warmth of her office in 43 Knollwood, however, Lauren's outlook improved. She warmed her feet on the radiator, sipped her coffee, and unfolded the newspaper. It was *The New York Times*, of course. Lauren was not inclined to read the whining student articles written for *The Pug Post*, Eaton's student newspaper. She wanted to enjoy this restorative me-time before embarking on her busy day.

And today looked particularly busy. The election for department chair was that afternoon, and Lauren knew she'd have to work to achieve her desired outcome. It was important that both Walter and Peter thought she was voting for them. Each man would need her attention and charm today. A quiet conversation over coffee, perhaps. An alluring perch on the edge of a desk. Lauren didn't care who won the election. She was only concerned that the winner would want to repay her for her support.

9:37 a.m.

Charles Covington III eased down into the desk chair in his small office at the back of 41 Knollwood Place. He closed his eyes and wallowed in the silence. Mildred, Charles's wife, had a lot to say these days. He had come to work for a rest.

Charles blamed Charlotte for this change in his wife. Charlotte, the college-aged daughter Charles fathered during an affair two decades ago, had only been an active part of the family for the last six months. In an effort to bond, she'd taken Mildred to a woman's seminar at the local library, and Mildred had embraced her emancipation. Gone were her flowery dresses, home-cooked meals, and quilting bees. Mildred now dressed in pant suits, wanted to discuss the political op-eds she read in *The New York Times*, and insisted she and Charles take their marriage to a new level.

This was why, after more than sixty years together, Charles and Mildred now went to couples therapy every week. Charles was learning a book's worth of pithy sayings—*out with frustration and in with love*—and even more about his wife's proclivities. He could have coped if Mildred had limited her conversations about needs and desires to their therapy hour. But it seemed she wanted to talk about liberation, self-worth, and erotic expression for most of the day and some of the night. Charles was exhausted and beginning to feel quite inadequate as a husband. Could it be that Mildred needed a younger man? Just the memory of their conversation in bed that morning made him blush. It was too much information.

Change your thoughts and you change your world! echoed the therapist in his mind. But Charles didn't have the energy to change his thoughts. That morning he felt every one of his eighty-eight years. It certainly hadn't helped that he'd walked by Lauren Masters on his way into school. She looked about sixteen and had stared straight through him like he was a ghost. It seemed that even the Economics Department, though pleasantly quiet, was making him feel elderly and deficient.

Perhaps he shouldn't vote today in the election for department chair. *Would he even be alive for the duration of the chair's term?* And it wasn't as if his vote even mattered. From Charles's perspective, the choices were Peter, the harmless worm, or Walter, the conniving and lethal scorpion. Charles had lived long enough that he'd seen both regimes in his time. The spineless leader that was crushed by his opinionated and demanding subjects. And the power hungry leader who ate all those below him. Charles didn't fancy either candidate, and the fact that both men were many years younger than Charles didn't help.

He harrumphed into his mustache. *Believe you can and you're halfway there,* chanted the therapist's voice. *What a load of...* Charles stopped mid-thought. Maybe the therapist was right. Maybe he just needed to believe in his own value. It made economic sense. Economies thrived when confidence was high. Charles sat up straighter in his chair and forgot his fatigue. His age wasn't a problem. It was an asset.

I'll make a run for chair myself, thought Charles

with increasing enthusiasm. *It's time for a little experience at the helm. And it would be a great excuse to spend more time away from Mildred and her "needs."*

9:41 a.m.

Peter Johansson did not consider himself a great man. In his early fifties, he had no illusions about the allure of his balding head and scrawny body to the opposite sex. Despite his mother's optimism each October, he knew he'd never win a Nobel Prize. And he understood that he didn't command the respect of his colleagues in the Economics Department at Eaton University. He'd been hired on the basis of one seminal publication and hadn't shined since.

To be sure, he was the most prolific publisher in the department. But as Walter Scovill was quick to point out, Peter's subsequent publications were in *field* journals. The way Walter said it, you'd think these were pieces of scrap paper torn to shreds by field mice as they made bedding for their young. As opposed to being peer-reviewed publications in a particular field of research, industrial organization in Peter's case. According to Walter Scovill, the only relevant count in the research game was the number of publications one had in the journals *of note*, the *American Economic Review* and *Journal of Political Economy*. Using that metric, Peter had scored only once, compared to Walter's twenty-three.

Peter knew his lack of greatness had been the sole reason he'd been appointed acting chair of the department after the debacle of last semester's murders. His colleagues wanted a placeholder until things returned to normal, and saw in him the perfect puppet. At the time, he'd accepted the job unwillingly. Being in charge of a department of academic prima donnas seemed like a thankless task. However, now that he'd tasted the power of his new position, Peter had no plans to give up the chairmanship. He wasn't a natural politician, and the reality of vote-begging made him uncomfortable. But the election was being held in five hours, and Peter was going to work until the last minute to ensure a win.

Peter Johannson double checked that he had his keys and then shut the door to his office in 43 Knollwood. Too many times, he'd pulled shut his door with the lock engaged and locked himself out of his office. He didn't have time to wait for the maintenance department to unlock his office today.

As he crossed the street, a determined-looking C.J. Whitmore strode towards him.

"Morning, Peter," she called out without slowing down. "I've lined up James Brimmage to do a seminar."

"Good work," he replied. "Is he in his office?"

"In all his glory."

Peter turned and called back to C.J. as she passed him. "Um, don't forget the vote this afternoon."

C.J. waved her hand in acknowledgement. *One vote secured,* Peter thought. *Let's see if I can get a second.* Minutes later, Peter knocked on James's office door and opened it half-way. "Mind if I come in?"

James waved him in. After C.J. had left, James had clicked on his computer and brought up a favorite website. It had some cutesy name, but Hot Girls in Tight Wet T-shirts would have been descriptive. James considered himself a guy with standards and didn't look at the full-frontal nude websites while in the office. He restricted himself to girls in wet t-shirts, girls in bikinis, and girls mud-wrestling. It was good to enjoy life, but also important to have boundaries. James didn't shut down his computer when Peter came into the room.

Peter nervously ran his hand over his scalp as he sat down in the uncomfortable wooden chair opposite James's desk. "Well, how's the Ducati? Going out for a spin today?" he asked in an awkward attempt to make conversation. James looked at Peter, looked out the window at the thick wall of snow that was falling, and then looked back at Peter.

"No," he said. "No. I don't think I'll be riding the motorcycle today." James often wondered about the personal lives of guys like Peter—the complete losers with no social skills. Had Peter ever had sex? And if so, how? And with what?

Peter started his spiel about the election for department chair and why he, Peter, would be the best candidate. He'd be fair in allocating department duties. He would be fiscally responsible. He would listen to the concerns of his colleagues. James tuned Peter out and went back to looking at his computer screen. *Enjoy life now.*

"Hmm," murmured James after a few minutes.

Peter, taking encouragement from this, kept talking.

"I see," muttered James, scrolling through pictures of busty women in all-white outfits, who apparently couldn't get out of the way of their sprinkler systems. "That *is* interesting."

"I'm glad you think so," agreed Peter, who continued to make his case for the upcoming election.

"Quite," said James, not listening.

"So," concluded Peter, "can I count on your support this afternoon?"

A silence hung in the air. James, becoming aware that Peter was looking at him expectantly, fumbled for an answer to the question he hadn't heard. "I…think so.

Yes. That…seems…reasonable? What do you think?"

"What do I think? I'm delighted to hear it. And rest assured, I'll do my best to help you as you transition into Eaton and its ways."

Peter stood up, shook hands with a mystified James, and left the office. James wondered briefly what he'd just agreed to and then went back to his computer.

9:43 a.m.

C.J. knew she should be thrilled to have another female on staff, but somehow she couldn't get excited about Lauren Masters. C.J. had met many Laurens in her time. The one-size-pleases-most girl at the party who'd talk football with the jock, quilting with the grandmother, trade recipes with the host, and flirt with the husbands. Maybe it was Lauren's giggling that annoyed C.J., or her tendency to bat her heavily made-up eyelids at her male colleagues. Or perhaps it was that Lauren wasn't that excited about C.J. *Too many hens in the henhouse,* thought C.J., berating herself. Trying to shake off her unfriendly attitude, she knocked gently on Lauren's office door. Not hearing any reply, C.J. knocked again, this time more loudly.

"Come in!" called an upbeat voice.

C.J. opened the door and leaned into the room. "Hello? Lauren?"

Lauren's welcoming demeanor dropped. "Oh. It's you." Lauren had been expecting James Brimmage, given their assignation the night before. She figured James would drop around "so there'd be no hard feelings." As if she cared at all about his feelings.

For Lauren, the previous night had been a career investment. She would cash in last night's chips when she needed something from James. For now, she would be the perfect one-night stand. No recriminations. No expectations. But when she wanted his assistance—for example, if the department were to vote on her promotion or she needed a colleague to take on her arduous committee work—Lauren would throw in a few veiled references to "their special night." A couple of meaningful glances in the faculty lounge, and James Brimmage would begin thinking about their acrobatic and rather steamy night together. The mere hope of doing it again would make him compliant to her wishes. What a windfall for one mediocre night. A much better investment than years of time-intensive research.

"Yes. It's just me, I'm afraid," said C.J., unable to keep the sarcasm out of her voice. C.J. couldn't help noticing that the only two items on Lauren's desk were *The New York Times* and a coffee mug. There were no lecture notes, no journal articles, no sign at all of any work being done. Unusual for a junior professor on a tenure time crunch. *Oh well,* thought C.J. *Not my problem.* "I wanted to chat with you about the seminar schedule. Somehow, I've landed the job of coordinating the speakers."

"I'm a little busy right now," Lauren said, as she opened the arts section of the newspaper to the crossword. "How about we meet for lunch and you can tell me all about it? I was planning to eat at Antonio's at midday."

C.J. breathed in deeply and forced out a smile. "Sounds lovely."

9:53 a.m.

Left alone, Lauren sipped her coffee and started

filling in answers to the crossword puzzle. She laughed quietly at the clue *Demanding subj,* and wrote in *ECON* as the answer. She struggled briefly with *GRE practice (PREP)* as she hadn't done any preparation before taking her graduate record examination. And she slowed to a near-stop with 38-down, *1993 Nobel winner.* The answer was five letters long. 1993? That was the year that Nelson MANDELA (*seven letters, not the correct answer*) had won the peace prize. And Toni MORRISON (*eight letters, even worse*) had received the Nobel Prize in literature.

Lauren lamented her slow time for the easy Monday-level crossword, blaming her reduced mental processing on C.J.'s unwanted interruption. There had been no justification for C.J. coming in person to ask about that stupid seminar schedule, when email would suffice. That was the problem with the middle-aged. They couldn't keep pace with technology.

Technology! Lauren thought, suddenly remembering Robert FOGEL has been awarded the 1993 Nobel in economics, for his research on railroads. As she filled in the answer, Lauren heard a knock at her door.

She smiled coyly to herself. This time it was sure to be James Brimmage. She ignored the knock and answered another clue (*Very, very old—ANCIENT; though,* Lauren mused, *COVINGTON would also be a great answer*). It was never a good idea to be too eager.

The person at the door knocked again.

Lauren looked up from the newspaper. "Come in!" she called out in a friendly voice. The door opened, and Lauren's visitor entered the room.

A few minutes later, Lauren Masters was slumped over her desk—dead.

TEN O'CLOCK

10:03 a.m.

Walter Scovill believed the best pedagogical practice was to teach the most irrelevant and esoteric material on the first day of class. The benefits of this system were indisputable. It scared off the dullards, reducing the amount of time he wasted re-explaining material in office hours. It impressed the Mensa members in the classroom, raising his teaching evaluation at the end of semester. And, most importantly, it elicited the female students who were happy to bat their eyelids for an *A*. They inevitably knocked at his office door, flirting for mercy, and increasing the pleasure component of the semester to an acceptable level.

He had struck upon this piece of wisdom early in his career and had never wavered from it. Walter didn't know the exact number of his colleagues who also adopted it, but he feared too few—judging from the cotton-candy style introductory lectures he'd overheard in past years. *Really*, he thought in disgust. *Who cares what students think the definition of economics is? It's not like they're actually going to redefine the subject.*

At just after ten o'clock, Walter Scovill walked into the classroom in the basement of 40 Knollwood. The previous professor—Arthur Fleitman—had left over twenty minutes earlier. Teaching was just another thing Arthur despised, and so he spent as little time as possible doing it. Arthur had, however, left the board covered with barely decipherable notes on the theories of microeconomic markets and Marshallian demand.

Walter, glancing at the blackboard, conceded a grudging respect to whomever had taught the hour before him. The material on the board was challenging, and there was no sign anyone had frittered away time with introductory fluff. The hard-to-read writing looked vaguely familiar, but Walter couldn't identify the scribe. *Maybe it was James Brimmage's class?* thought Walter, unsure of anyone else's teaching schedule. *You can never tell with foreigners. Sometimes they're decent.*

Walter stomped the snow off his boots. He'd opted against using the Smythe Lounge to get from his office to the classroom, hoping the cold would temper his cocaine crash. Still edgy, however, he eyed the full classroom of waiting students. *Stop breathing my oxygen,* Walter thought, as he placed a pile of papers on the desk at the front of the room and paused to sniff the air. The room smelt vaguely like a low-rent ski lodge— an unpleasant mix of soggy fleece, deodorant, and the previous night's party being sweated out of pubescent pores. Walter beckoned a student sitting in the front row. "Erase these notes," he said, pointing to the blackboard. "I need to use the board for class today."

Walter's class was an upper-level undergraduate macroeconomics class, and the enrollment numbers were capped at sixty. There was currently a waiting list, but Walter wasn't worried. There would be fewer than twenty students in the class after today's lecture.

"This is Advanced Macroeconomics. My name is Professor Scovill. If you aren't meant to be in this class, you're in the wrong place and, frankly, you're stupid. A five-year-old can comprehend a college timetable."

There was an awkward shuffling in the middle of the classroom. A tall, slender boy, blushing red, stumbled out of the room.

"There's always one," said Walter, looking around the room. "No one else?"

The remaining students stayed seated.

"Very good. The stack of paper in front of me is the syllabus for the course. If you want to know about your test dates and textbook, I recommend that you take one before you leave. But that, of course, is up to you. Economics is about choice."

Walter often thought the students didn't realize this important fact. Economics wasn't principally about the stock market or taxes. These were just examples. Economics was about how to make a choice when you can't have everything. For example, at that moment Walter had to choose between being a popular professor and having the fewest students possible. He placed a high value on time, so that choice was easy.

"Let's get started. I'm told you are the best students in the country. If that is true, you should be able to follow along. If you can't, well, perhaps your admission here was a mistake."

Walter then began lecturing Ph.D. level material, drawn randomly from both micro- and macro-economics. It was subject matter that the advanced doctoral students struggled with. The undergraduates sitting in front of him had no hope of understanding. He quickly covered the freshly-cleaned board with complex mathematics and diagrams as he separated hyperplanes, disproved the Phillips curve, optimized a Bellman dynamic programming equation, and proved Walras' Law.

Walter looked around the room and smiled to himself. The students were scribbling notes frenetically. The openly stupid ones looked completely overwhelmed. Those convinced of their own intellectual acumen couldn't follow along either, but were nodding as if they understood. No one would raise a hand to ask him to slow down or explain the material further. That would be equivalent to admitting they weren't Eaton-quality. Most would prefer to drop the course instead of risking ridicule or a low grade. Walter could see the panicked faces. *Good*, he thought with satisfaction. *There will be no issue of a waiting list.*

He took the time to peruse the stock of co-eds, assessing those likely to beg for their *A*. Walter was not an attractive man. He'd spent his middle age gaining pounds and losing hair. However, what he lacked in looks he made up for in confidence and testosterone. Even without the benefit of his cocaine-high, he felt like a bull in musth. He loathed students, but loved a firm, bouncy, limber co-ed. *I should get at least three knocking at my door by the end of the week,* he thought happily.

10:08 a.m.

Mary Beth Sanders finished another episode of *Say Yes to the Dress*. It was, like, so unfair. Some of the brides-to-be were hideously ugly, horribly fat, and had never made the time for a manicure. But they were shopping for wedding dresses, so obviously a man had proposed to them. Who were these men? Where were these men? And why hadn't one of them proposed to Mary Beth?

In the last episode, one future bride looked as if she'd accidently fallen asleep in a tanning bed for the last twenty years, while her hair soaked in a bowl of bleach. And she'd clearly landed a Mr. Rich, judging from the photos they displayed of her and a grandpa-dude on vacation in the Bahamas.

Mary Beth sighed. *Say Yes to the Dress* really helped

clarify her life goals. Mary Beth knew she would, like, literally die if she didn't get married in a Pnina Tornai wedding dress. There was no way she was going to settle for some cheap $5000 imitation. You had to start a marriage how you intended to keep going—encased in designer silk, diamonds, and Swarovski crystals.

Mary Beth sighed again as she closed her Netflix account. Without the excuse of Mr. Rich, she had to get back to work. Apparently, it was her job to inform the recent hires about the diversity training for new faculty that was taking place later today, and to make sure they attended. Somehow, she'd missed that email. It had been quite a surprise when the snippy person from human resources had called a few minutes ago to see why Mary Beth hadn't RSVPed on behalf of the new faculty.

"Training?" Mary Beth had asked, confused, her attention still focused on the final scene of *Say Yes to the Dress*. The tanning-bed lady had chosen a ruched, mermaid-style gown with crystal and pearl beading. "Like, at the gym?" Mary Beth had seen no reason for the woman from human resources to be quite so rude in her reply. *What do you want me to do, lady? Read all the long, boring-looking emails in my inbox?*

Mary Beth decided to break the news to Lauren Masters first. That way, she could reward herself afterwards with a visit to Professor Brimmage's office. She printed out the email that the grumpy human resources lady had grudgingly re-sent. It was much easier to read an email than remember it. Recalling small details wasn't Mary Beth's forte. She looked over at Lauren's still-uncopied photocopying before heading out. *If she asks, I'll tell her I've been super busy, working on some important department stuff for Professor Johansson.*

Mary Beth teetered across Knollwood Place,

slipping on the icy street in her high-heeled boots. She cursed the winter weather, her faux fur boots, and the lack of underpass between the buildings on the opposite side of Knollwood Place. After her third skid on the ice, Mary Beth added a vacation home in Maui to her requirements for Mr. Rich Husband. *And it better be a nice vacation home. Not some tacky condo,* she thought, her mood not improved by the cold wind whipping up her short skirt. Mary Beth wanted true beach front, with banana loungers, lots of palm trees, and an infinity pool. *Complete with pool boy,* she added, picturing herself having a tanned, well-muscled man attend to her every need while she sunbathed in her bikini.

Mary Beth stumbled up the stairs to 43 Knollwood, skidding on the gravelly piles of ice melt that had been spread by the maintenance crew. Rather ungracefully, her heel caught on the door sill and she lurched through the front entrance of the building. She looked around to see if anyone had witnessed her awkward arrival. Thankfully, no one was about. She composed herself in front of Lauren's office door, straightening her clothes and inwardly rehearsing her little speech. *Sorry to disturb you. Today at one o'clock you have*, Mary Beth paused to look down at the printed email she was carrying, *"Empathy and Sensitivity Training: Creating an Inclusive and Diverse Workplace." I, like, thought I should tell you in person, as it's important and you have to go.*

Mary Beth paused, entertaining the idea of telling Lauren the training began at two o'clock, or not telling her at all. It was tempting. The thought of Lauren Masters and James Brimmage confined in the same room together was unsettling. None of the women on *Say Yes to the Dress* ever mentioned having to outshine someone like Lauren Masters.

I can't not tell her, Mary Beth thought glumly. *It's*

impossible to keep secrets in this department. Professor Brimmage or Professor Fleitman will talk to her about it, for sure.

Without enthusiasm, Mary Beth knocked on Lauren's door. Lauren didn't answer. Mary Beth knocked again, this time a little louder. Still Lauren didn't answer. Mary Beth tried the handle. It was locked.

Well, I tried. It's not my fault if she doesn't know about the training, thought Mary Beth, conveniently forgetting the contribution of her own unread emails to the last-minute nature of her news. *I bet she hasn't even arrived for work today. And she wanted me to rush her photocopying. Well, good luck. That toothpick-art-project will be lucky if I get to her photocopying before spring break.*

10:17 a.m.

C.J. Whitmore sat in her office in 42 Knollwood, looking disconsolately at her computer screen. There were so many things she should be doing: writing a referee's report, reviewing her lecture notes, analyzing the data for her latest research, recruiting more seminar participants. The list seemed endless. But she couldn't find the motivation to do any of it. Her productivity had been dampened by the black mood her meeting with Lauren Masters had induced. *Women like her were the reason men didn't have any respect for the opposite sex.*

C.J. chided herself. *That wasn't fair. She barely knew the woman. Besides, Lauren wasn't nearly as vacuous as Mary Beth Sanders.* C.J. paused. *Maybe that was the problem. Lauren was smart enough to know better.*

Still feeling irritated, C.J. aimlessly clicked open her email, hoping the pretense of productivity would induce the real thing. *Fake it 'til you make it*, she thought, and then stared at her inbox. Two hundred forty-two new emails? Since eight that morning? Who were these people?

A quick glance through the messages revealed the problem. The IT department had sent an email to every faculty member in the university about the upcoming service outage on Sunday morning at 2:00 a.m. And some idiot from the Political Science Department, Professor Jason Someone, had written a snarky message back about not overfilling his valuable inbox. C.J. actually agreed with the man. She didn't inform the IT department of her work schedule. She saw no reason for them to tell her. The problem was that Jason had hit "reply all."

This triggered a tsunami of correspondence. Some professors replied to the entire list, saying "don't use reply all." Others just chimed in with their personal views about the IT department. The IT department sent their own response, defending their policy of informing the faculty of all events. Finally, a rather irate full professor from the Business School sent an email with the subject line, "NO ONE CARES WHAT YOU THINK," effectively bringing the exchange to an end.

Just as she was about to delete her entire inbox, one message caught C.J.'s attention. It wasn't part of the IT conversation. Rather, it was from an administrator in the Dean's office, asking for nominations for a teaching award. Teaching awards were a delicate matter. Faculty were promoted based on their research records. To be worthy of a teaching award meant you'd been wasting your time.

C.J.'s Ph.D. advisor had actually boasted about his

poor teaching evaluations. "I'm an academic," he always said when challenged over his abilities in the classroom. "If you wanted a teacher, you should have hired one." C.J. understood the rationale. Economic theory posited the benefits of occupational specialization. No one expected the astronauts to clean the bathrooms at NASA headquarters. Why would you ask a research scientist to teach?

But this award was open to anyone. C.J. thought of Betsy Williams. The woman was an adjunct—and so not expected to research—and a dedicated teacher. Betsy taught the classes that the tenured faculty wouldn't touch. Macro for the masses, as it were. She might enjoy the recognition of her work.

C.J. read the email again. To be successful, the nominee needed endorsements from at least three tenured faculty members. *Three?* Hoping that wasn't going to be too high a hurdle, C.J. composed a new email message to the tenured faculty members in the Economics Department.

TO: Tenured Faculty
FROM: C.J. Whitmore
SUBJECT: Betsy Williams Teaching Award
We have the opportunity to nominate Betsy Williams for a teaching award. I know we all appreciate her efforts in the classroom, and I think this would be a nice acknowledgement.

She needs three recommendations from tenured faculty. I would be happy to write one. Who else would like to?

C.J.

A few minutes later, C.J.'s email pinged to signal incoming mail.

TO: Tenured Faculty
FROM: Peter Johannson
SUBJECT: RE: Betsy Williams Teaching Award

Thanks for highlighting this, C.J. I would be delighted to write a recommendation for Betsy. She is a true asset to the department.

Best,

Peter

Message sent from my iPhone

C.J. was pleased to get such a quick response, but prickled at Peter's overt flattery. Betsy was good at her job, but "true asset" was a bit strong. It sounded like a last-minute play for votes.

What is wrong with me? C.J. wondered at her negative mood. *Not every egg in the nest is rotten.* Peter couldn't have been after Betsy's vote. Betsy wasn't even allowed to vote in today's election. It was faculty only. There was no reason for her to doubt Peter's sincerity. And it wasn't as if the reason behind his endorsement mattered anyway. With her and Peter on board, she only needed one more full professor to endorse Betsy. Charles was a good bet. He'd known Betsy since she was a student at Eaton.

C.J. glanced at Peter's email one last time. *Message sent from my iPhone.* She didn't understand why people who owned ten-thousand-dollar computers and could touch type chose to peck out messages on a five-inch screen. It wasn't very efficient. And wasn't that what economics was all about?

10:20 a.m.

Betsy was teaching Introduction to Microeconomics for the second time that morning. Economics was a popular major among the dollar-motivated Eaton undergraduates, so this semester she was teaching the same class at four different times. Betsy glanced at the clock. Exactly twenty minutes past the hour. She was right on time. The students were passing their surveys down to the front, and it was time to begin a class brainstorm on the definition of economics.

Betsy silently signaled her desire for the students' attention by raising her right arm in the air. She tried to avoid yelling at her class for quiet, as the juxtaposition of a screeched request for silence always struck her as absurd. It took a few minutes, but she soon had the attention of those before her.

"Thank you for taking the time to fill out the survey. To begin our lecture today, we're going to define the term *economics*."

Betsy turned to the blackboard, and wrote ECONOMICS in large letters across the center. As she wrote, she noticed a dark spot on the skin above her wrist. *What was that? And how long had it been there?* Betsy made a mental note to Google her latest symptom (*could it possibly be a skin cancer?)* and then turned her attention back to the class.

"What is economics?" Betsy asked the students.

An uncomfortable silence followed. No one wanted to get such a basic question wrong. Betsy noticed a few students tapping their cell phones. A preppy boy in the front row raised his hand. "The study of production, consumption, and the transfer of wealth."

Before the arrival of her iPad, Betsy had always been impressed with this answer to her definition question. In recent years, it was frequently the first answer offered and Betsy had attributed this to a rise in the number of students who read the textbook before class. However, she now realized it was the top entry of the Google search for "definition of economics." She jotted the words *production, consumption,* and *wealth* on the blackboard.

"But what do these words actually mean? What are

we going to learn in this class?" she prompted.

The class was silent, and several students began tapping on their phones again. Betsy assumed they were Googling for other answers, though she realized they could just be texting their friends or checking ESPN. The actions were observationally equivalent.

"There's no wrong answer," Betsy encouraged. "I just want to know what economics means to you."

Silence resettled around the room. Betsy waited the students out.

"It's about making money," a student sitting in the middle of the lecture hall finally said.

"Thank you," Betsy effused, as she wrote *making money* on the board.

Other students, made brave by Betsy's enthusiasm, decided they had better definitions.

"It tells you how much to charge for stuff."

"What happens if you don't charge the right amount?" Betsy asked.

"You go bankrupt."

Betsy jotted down *bankruptcy* on the blackboard.

"Economics is more than prices," a budding entrepreneur added. "It's about how to run the entire business."

Betsy added *running a business* to the board.

"It's how to run a country and not have everyone unemployed."

"Yeah. You need to know it to become President," added a future politician.

Betsy wrote busily on the blackboard, surrounding the word ECONOMICS with their ideas.

"Taxes!" one student yelled out.

"And how to avoid them," added another trust funder.

Betsy was amazed how similar the definition of economics was from class to class, even after the students moved beyond their internet answers. Her earlier class that day had decided, after their brainstorming session, that they would define economics as "the art of making money."

10:32 a.m.

To optimize his mental stimulation, intellectual growth, and, frankly, money-earning potential, James Brimmage worked for two one-hour blocks every day. He restricted the length of each work block to one hour, as both his rate of productivity and enjoyment fell when boredom set in. And, after some initial experimentation, James had found just two hours of focused work a day had been sufficient to ensure his tenure at elite institutions such as Duke, and now Eaton.

It was true that working more hours a day could potentially result in higher accolades. If James was honest, he wasn't likely to win the Nobel Prize, though the possibility couldn't be discounted altogether. But when he'd performed the cost-benefit analysis of *definitely* increasing his workload for only the *possibility* of awards and glory, he quickly calculated that extended work hours were for suckers.

Consequently, every morning between ten and eleven, and every afternoon between one and two, James gave his full concentration to the world of economics. At these times, he didn't answer email; he didn't surf the web; he even avoided sexting. During these two hours, the only thing he did was economic research.

On this particular Monday, half an hour into his morning work slot, James was consumed with the issue of intertemporal price discrimination. He had two computers going, using one to run computer code and the other to type up results. His desk was a sea of printed paper, and his ears were covered by Bose noise-cancelling headphones

Knock-knock.

James heard the knock on his door as the Bose headphones were not actually noise-cancelling. They were merely noise-reducing. James ignored the person at the door and continued to think about the implications of intertemporal price discrimination in health insurance markets, using randomized stochastic frontier modeling. *This is such a simple problem,* he berated himself. *I should have it solved by now.* Frustrated, he looked up from his computer screens and stared at the door, hoping for inspiration. Astounded, he noticed the handle turning and the door beginning to open. *God damn these elitist, Northeastern, entitled, intrusive...*

"I'm not here!" he exploded.

A young woman dressed in a carnage of faux animal skins teetered into the room.

"Yoo-hoo, Professor Brimmage. It's me, Mary Beth."

James sighed, removing his headphones. A man has to have standards, and even James wouldn't lower himself to the likes of Mary Beth—a woman dolled up in cheap clothes and drenched in the scent of desperation. James was perfectly aware that since he'd arrived at Eaton, four months ago, she'd been trying her best to land him as a husband. James shuddered at the thought. He liked women but had no interest in a wife.

Mary Beth sashayed over to his desk and perched on the edge. "I hope this isn't a bad time."

James, not wanting to encourage conversation, just glared back.

"It's just that I, like, have to make sure you go to this

important thing. It's amanda-something. I forget the exact word. It means, you know, like you have to go."

"Mandatory?"

"That's the word," Mary Beth cooed. "Aren't you clever?"

James stayed silent.

"Don't you want to know what you have to go to?" Mary Beth teased.

"Not really," said James curtly. Minutes were ticking by in his work hour, and his temper was not improving.

"Oh, you silly. Sure you do. It's," Mary Beth looked down at her printed email, "Empathy and Sensitive Training: Creating an Inclusive and Diverse Workplace."

"Bloody hell. Sounds like crap. When is it?"

"Well, I guess I should've told you earlier, but it's at one o'clock this afternoon. Over in…"

James cut her off. "Email me the details. I'll be there," he lied. One o'clock was the start of his second work hour, and James Brimmage had no intention of rearranging his schedule. "I assume I'm not being singled out for this punishment. Do all new professors have to go?"

"Oh, yes," Mary Beth frowned slightly. *All new professors? Like Lauren Masters?* She leaned in closer to give James a good view of his alternative.

He stood up abruptly, as way of dismissal. "Thank you, Mary Beth. You can close the door on your way out."

James put back on his headphones and settled back into his work. Mary Beth's seductive bottom wiggle, offered as a goodbye wave as she walked out, was completely wasted as James was already staring back at the double computer screens.

10:34 a.m.

After his nine a.m. class, Arthur Fleitman had returned to his office in 40 Knollwood to recover from the morning exertion of teaching. He'd stretched out on a very comfortable, dark brown leather La-Z-Boy recliner, rested a magazine on his stomach, and closed his eyes. The recliner was not on the list of things that Arthur despised. In contrast to most things in his life, he was very fond of it and had arranged its delivery to his office only hours after joining the department at Eaton. *Not too hard. Not too soft.* The recliner was an integral part of Arthur's work day, and he intended to stay thus reclined, pretending to read a magazine while enjoying his mid-morning nap, until his lunchtime at midday.

A knock at his office door caused Arthur to open his eyes. "Go away!" he yelled unceremoniously.

His office door opened, and a woman in hot pink cowboy boots strode in.

"What part of *go away* didn't you understand?" he asked C.J. Whitmore grumpily, while levering his La-Z-Boy to the sitting position.

"The part where you didn't make nice, since you were so kind to ask," C.J. snarked back. She was still not in the best of moods. On her way to Arthur's office, she hadn't been able to avoid Mary Beth, who'd been prowling around the corridors of 42 Knollwood. Hoping to pass without having a conversation, C.J. had barely nodded a hello. Mary Beth hadn't taken the hint.

"Hi, Professor Whitmore," Mary Beth had said, stopping to talk. "I haven't seen any of your students yet."

C.J. had looked confused. *Why would her students need to see Mary Beth?*

Mary Beth responded by wriggling her brilliant green fingernails in C.J.'s face. "You know, the ones that, like, need a little inspiration."

C.J. nodded, finally understanding. *The all-powerful manicure.* It was distinctly possible that a chicken—with its head removed—would have a greater intellectual capacity than Mary Beth.

"I guess it's because I've been out of the office a bit this morning," Mary Beth added. "Assisting, and the like."

Mary Beth toodled a fingernail wave as she sashayed away (*presumably to hunt down James Brimmage,* C.J. thought), and C.J. internally apologized to Lauren Masters. No matter what Lauren said or did, she could never be as irritating as Mary Beth.

Now, in Arthur's office, C.J. tried to squash her ill-temper. As her father used to say, "Better to ignore a flea bite than scratch it."

"If you can break yourself away from..." C.J. glanced over at the magazine that was still resting on Arthur's lap, "...the *Yachting Times,* perhaps we can discuss the possibility of you presenting a seminar in the department."

High on Arthur's list of dislikes were seminars. He loathed attending them. Nothing was more boring than listening to economists drone on about inconsequential research that they'd wasted months of time and countless thousands of grant dollars undertaking. He always asked the same question. *Why do we care about this?* And the presenter generally fumbled for an answer. *Well, because, you see, the methodological implications could be carried over to other areas...it's possible the results can be extrapolated to alternative economic scenarios...there's a chance that the paper sheds insight into the economic consumer's rationale.* Arthur had one reply to all this self-justifying mumbo-jumbo, and it wasn't a word he would say in front of a lady.

And as for presenting a seminar...Arthur Fleitman had no desire to be one of the things he most disliked— a tedious waste of time. "Young lady, it appears you don't understand the field of economics that well. A valuable resource is a scarce resource. If I made my thoughts and research freely available any time anyone asked, I'd lower the value of my research. So, no. I will not present a seminar this semester. And if you valued your career, you'd follow my lead." Arthur levered his La-Z-Boy back to the reclining position and started flicking through his yachting magazine, pointedly ignoring C.J.

C.J. narrowed her eyes at the old man. *There was more than one way to skin the proverbial cat.* "You're absolutely right. I'd been hoping you'd present the Whitley seminar, but I see now such a request is impossible. Your scarcity, and your value, must be preserved. I guess I'll just have to make Lauren Masters the feature seminar speaker for this semester. I'm meeting her for lunch, and I'll ask her then."

C.J. stopped talking, and waited.

Arthur Fleitman turned the pages of the magazine slowly, his thin lips pushed into a frown.

C.J. whistled to herself and looked absently out the window of Arthur's office onto Knollwood Place. She noticed Peter Johansson walking down the street.

Arthur continued to thumb through his magazine.

C.J. sincerely hoped that Peter would be re-elected chair of the department today. She didn't think she could bear another three years of tyranny under Walter.

"Fine," Arthur finally said ungraciously, levering himself up to a sitting position again.

C.J. smiled. She knew the carrot of the most prestigious seminar given at Eaton during the course of the year was too much for Arthur Fleitman, or any academic, to resist. It would be attended by the best economists from all over the East coast, including those at Princeton whom Arthur despised. For that reason alone, C.J. had been confident that Arthur would accept the opportunity.

"I'll do the seminar as a favor to you," said Arthur. "We both know that pathetic excuse for a junior professor couldn't do the Whitley seminar. Her very existence here is a stain on my reputation."

C.J. ignored Arthur's slander of Lauren, preferring to wait until she had coffee with Betsy Williams before she expressed her thoughts on that subject. "You've made me happier than a pig in a cornfield," she said— somewhat truthfully—as her irritable mood lifted slightly with the victory. "I'll email you the details." She clicked out of Arthur's office, and he reclined back into his chair, a painful grimace on his face. Arthur Fleitman added Texas, Texans, and, in particular, manipulative women from the Lone Star state, to the list of things he despised.

10:41 a.m.

About forty minutes into his lecture, Walter paused and looked around the classroom. It was, he had to admit, invigorating to know he had the power to create such misery. What had they said in rehab? *The only person who can make you happy is you.* He chuckled to himself. He was doing a great job at that today. And it would only get better when he won the election that afternoon.

"That's enough for today," he told the class. "It is, after all, just the first day of class. We'll leave the challenging material for the next lecture."

Walter smiled and adopted a pseudo-helpful tone.

"Education is like a train journey. You don't go anywhere if you're not on board. If you missed the train today, now is the time to drop this class. If you need some help with the material," and here Walter looked pointedly at the three attractive girls he'd picked out, "you should come and see me this afternoon. You don't want to miss the ride."

Leaving behind a classroom of bewildered and panicked students, Walter hummed to himself as he walked back to his office through the empty Smythe Lounge. Energized, he pulled out his smartphone to check for messages. He had almost three hundred new emails. *A classic example of the overuse of free goods,* he thought. *People should have to pay for every email they send. Spam would become nonexistent.* He glanced at the most recent messages and saw C.J.'s plea for a teaching award for Betsy Williams, along with Peter's reply. *Spare me the participation ribbons,* he thought.

> *TO: Tenured Faculty*
> *FROM: Walter Scovill*
> *SUBJECT: RE: Betsy Williams Teaching Award*
> *There's a reason that the Nobel Prize in economics is not based on a person's teaching ability. Research is what matters. I would happily trade two Betsy Williamses for one decent research professor. If you value the reputation of this department, you would do the same.*
> *W.S.*

Having no doubt about the value of his own correspondence, Walter pressed send. *That'll round up any stray votes for the election this afternoon,* he thought. *Nothing like a show of force.*

10:46 a.m.

Arthur was just getting settled back into his mid-morning nap when another knock sounded at his door. Arthur, eyes closed and magazine resting comfortably across his belly, ignored it. Collegial visits were another thing Arthur hated. A college department wasn't supposed to resemble a prairie dog convention, with everyone popping in and out of neighboring offices every five minutes. Was it too much to expect everyone to stay quietly in their own space for an hour? He didn't care if they did any work. Arthur just wanted to be left alone.

The knock sounded at the door again.

"Go away!" Arthur yelled.

The door opened cautiously, and Mary Beth peered her head around. "Is this a bad time, Professor Fleitman?" she asked, mispronouncing his name *Flitman*.

Arthur, eyes still closed, recognized the voice and groaned. He hated stupid people.

Mary Beth interpreted his silence as consent and entered the room. "Oh, good. I was worried that I was disturbing you. It's just that, there's, like, this thing you have to go to this afternoon. And I need to tell you about it so I know that you know that you have to go." Mary Beth paused for a breath.

Arthur opened his eyes, levered into the sitting position, and groaned loudly.

"Are you feeling okay, Professor Fleitman?" Mary Beth asked, still managing to rhyme his name with *hitman*.

"Young lady, my name is not *Flitman*. It is Fleitman. The pronunciation is like *right man*. As in, 'Arthur Fleitman is the right man.'" He smiled slightly, amused at his play on words.

Mary Beth nodded. "Oh, I see. Flightman." Mary Beth wondered to herself how she'd gotten the spelling of Arthur's last name so wrong, but made a mental note to change it on all the documents in the office next time she was bored and looking for something to do. She stood in front of Arthur silently, rocking on her high heels, until frustration finally forced Arthur to ask, "Is there something you wanted to tell me?"

"About what?"

"I don't know. You're the one who came to see me." Mary Beth looked blankly at him.

"You mentioned something about a *thing* this afternoon."

"Oh. Yes." Mary Beth looked down at the piece of paper in her hand, pausing briefly to admire her nails. "You need to go to Empathy and Sensitivity Training: Creating an Inclusive and Diverse Workplace, today at one."

Not for the first time that day, Mary Beth wondered what *empathy* meant, and why the new faculty had to be trained in it. But it must be important, as the human resources woman had been very clear that it was her job to inform each new faculty member of the event, and make sure they understood they were required to be there.

"Do you understand, Professor Flightman?" Mary Beth finally asked, as Arthur hadn't replied.

"Yes."

"I can email you the location and everything. Or tell you now, if that's easier." Mary Beth wasn't sure if someone as old as Arthur knew how to use a computer.

"Don't bother. I'm not going."

"But, it's like, amanda-something."

"Young lady, if anyone asks you why I missed the *mandatory* Empathy and Sensitivity Training, you should feel free to tell them that I show tremendous empathy and sensitivity on a daily basis. As this university insists on diversifying my workplace with people who possess IQ's below 200, I am forced to include the dull and dimwitted into my life."

"Uh, okay," Mary Beth agreed.

"And," Arthur continued, not yet satisfied that he'd made his point, "if anyone had the slightest empathy and sensitivity for my sanity and my highly educated and acutely intelligent brain cells, they'd make it a personal priority to actively exclude the imbeciles, such as yourself, from my personal workspace."

With this, Arthur dismissed Mary Beth with a wave of his hand, and laid back down in his recliner. Mary Beth stared at him for a few moments.

"So," she began tentatively, "um, you know, you do have to, like, go to this training this afternoon."

"Get out!" yelled Arthur, without opening his eyes.

10:53 a.m.

Forgiveness is easier than permission, thought Charles Covington, as he finished his tumbler of gin. Since deciding to run for chair of the department an hour ago, he'd drunk slightly more than Mildred would have approved of. The first two glasses had been for courage. The third one was to show the young whippersnappers in the department who was boss. The last three were in celebration of his impending victory. The gin bottle which he kept in the bottom drawer of his desk was now empty.

Young people think they're so clever with their talk of natural highs from weed and mushrooms, thought Charles, remembering a recent conversation with Charlotte. He harrumphed into his moustache. That sort of talk didn't impress him. All he needed to bolster his enthusiasm and courage was the flavor of juniper berries.

He took another sip and thought more about the election. *I bet Arthur Fleitman would vote for me. He's old too. I'll go across to his office and chat with him about it.*

Minutes later, Charles, wearing his signature green polka dot bow tie and red suspenders, stumbled slightly as he walked up the stairs of 40 Knollwood. At the same time, Mary Beth came down the stairs from the second floor, smudging her tear-streaked mascara with a tissue.

"What's the matter, my dear?" asked Charles, as Mary Beth sniffed in his direction.

"Nothing," said Mary Beth in a small voice that implied that everything was wrong, but she was going to martyr through all her trials and tribulations.

"A burden shared is a burden lightened," said Charles, mimicking his therapist. *Unless,* he thought, *you have to listen to the drivel. Then a burden shared is a burden inherited.* Charles turned down his hearing aids.

"Well," whimpered Mary Beth pathetically, "since you've asked, that nasty Professor Flightman just yelled at me."

Charles nodded, not actually hearing a word she said.

"And that's not all," continued Mary Beth. "I had to see Professor Masters this morning about an important training. The training is at one this afternoon, and I'm going to be in, like, serious trouble if I don't tell her about it. But she didn't answer her door when I knocked. I guess not all of us start work before lunchtime." Mary Beth felt the immediate cheer of trashing Lauren Masters. It improved her mood every time.

Charles nodded again, glad to see Mary Beth had stopped crying.

"Have you seen her?" asked Mary Beth.

Charles nodded again, and seeing her expectant look, replied in vague (and hopefully appropriate) terms. "Of course. Wonderful, wonderful. It's always good to see a beautiful young lady smiling."

Charles was startled to see Mary Beth's pout returning. He excused himself quickly and hurried away to Arthur's office before the woman could start crying again. There was only so much comforting he could do. It was bad enough he had to listen to Mildred's grievances every day.

Charles knocked on Arthur's door. He had long ago stopped trying to listen for a reply. Even with his hearing aids on, he couldn't hear the sounds muffled by a heavy oak door. Charles tried the door handle and, finding the door unlocked, opened it and called out, "Hello? Arthur? It's Charles."

"Go away."

"Christmas Day?" Charles asked uncertainly, entering the room. "Mine was fine, thanks for asking. Not great, but decent, you understand. Just Mildred, Charlotte, and myself. Mildred's given up cooking, so we ordered in Chinese."

Arthur looked up from his La-Z-Boy. Any time he felt old, he just looked at Charles Covington III and realized *I'm not old. You are.* The man was a walking mausoleum, and half-living proof of the problem with the tenure system. Arthur considered explaining to Charles that he had never mentioned Christmas Day, but realized they'd both be a year older by the time he got the issue straightened out. Neither man had that sort of time to spare.

"Is there something I can do for you?"

Charles looked blankly at Arthur for a moment, and then remembered his hearing aids were still turned down. He adjusted them. "Say again?"

"Is there something I can do for you?" asked Arthur, as he levered into the sitting position. Arthur could smell the wafts of gin but said nothing. It was Arthur's personal motto not to start drinking until noon.

Charles sat down in a nearby wooden chair and harrumphed. "This chair is none too soft," he remarked.

"Is there something I can do for you?" repeated Arthur.

"Well, now," said Charles, "you know there's this election for chair this afternoon."

Arthur groaned. He hated office politics. "I know, and I don't care. I can't abide office politics. Walter? Peter? I don't plan on voting for either. So whichever one you're kingmaker for, please assure your boy that while I'm not voting for him, I won't vote against him. Think of me as Switzerland."

Charles cleared his throat. "Actually, I was thinking of entering the race and running for chair myself. The experienced candidate."

Arthur stared back at Charles. Arthur didn't like office politics, but he did enjoy a good show. And watching Walter Scovill and Peter Johansson scrabble for votes when Charles announced he was running would be highly entertaining. Every last vote would count.

"You know, Charles," said Arthur thoughtfully, "that's a fantastic idea. You have my vote, and I bet you'd get some other votes in the department as well. You get out there and start canvassing, my friend."

10:57 a.m.

Peter Johansson sat alone at a small wooden table in Wallaby's coffee shop. He'd emailed Lauren Masters earlier that morning to arrange an early coffee at ten-thirty. It was now almost eleven, and there was no sign of her. *Women,* he thought. *Why do they always run late?*

He sipped his grayish coffee, diluted from the original black by non-fat milk, and looked around the room. The typical assortment of Eaton students were perched at the coffee bar, lounging on the comfortable sofas, and waiting in line to charge extra-large-double-shot-lattes-with-whip to their parents' credit cards. No one looked particularly studious, but it was just the first day of semester.

"Peter!"

Peter looked up, on hearing his name. However, it wasn't Lauren Masters calling out, but Betsy Williams, the long-time adjunct teaching fellow for the department. Peter liked Betsy well enough, though he was fascinated how a woman with a Ph.D. from Eaton could achieve so little in her life. Just teach classes? No publications? It wasn't a life that would get Peter out of bed in the morning.

Betsy, a woman old enough to remember life before Peter was born and wise enough not to mention it, waddled her hefty frame towards Peter's table. "Happy first day of semester!" she said cheerfully, a large mocha latte in hand. "I'm early for my coffee date. Can I join you for a few minutes?"

"Of course," said Peter, always the gentleman. The woman, as an adjunct, had zero power, zero influence, and couldn't even vote in today's election for chair of the department. However, he had a new appreciation of Betsy after his short period being chair. The woman taught the introductory subjects that no tenured professor would touch, she never complained about her students, and she was willing to teach the classes scheduled before noon. He was happy to endorse her for a teaching award, if that kept her in the classroom. "It appears my coffee date has forgotten our meeting. I was supposed to be meeting Lauren Masters here at ten-thirty."

Betsy tsked her disapproval of Lauren and her thoughtlessness. "Isn't today your big day? The election?" asked Betsy.

"Yes. Only four hours to go. Speaking of which, if you'll excuse me, I should go and rally a few more voters. I'd hoped to secure Lauren's vote over coffee, but I guess I'll have to find her in the department."

"Of course, Peter. A pleasure seeing you."

As Peter left, Betsy reached for her new iPad. Previously an avid knitter, she'd forgone the knitting needles and crochet hooks for her post-Christmas internet obsession with WebMD and Facebook.

Betsy was fascinated by Facebook. She friended everyone, but never posted anything herself. She was the fly on the wall, watching everyone's lives. No one liked to refuse her friend requests. Who wanted to offend such a sweet old lady? But soon everyone forgot that she was watching. She'd quickly learned which grandchildren were smoking pot, which friends were having affairs, and which of the junior professors spent the week in the Hamptons when they said they were home sick.

Betsy clicked on Lauren's Facebook wall, wondering what Lauren Masters was doing that was so important she couldn't meet that nice Peter Johansson for coffee. According to her posts, Lauren had met friends for drinks two nights ago, she *liked* her hairdresser yesterday, and she had recently reconnected with an old flame. Just that morning, Lauren had posted a picture of herself doing *The New York Times* crossword puzzle, with the caption "Solving the problem of getting tenure."

Betsy sighed. She wondered how Lauren could be so glib about tenure. It only happened for those who worked very hard, and even then it wasn't guaranteed. From what Betsy had heard, Lauren didn't seem to be working that hard, or to be that worried. Look at how she'd blown off a meeting with Peter, the potential chair of the department—and for no apparent reason judging from her Facebook page. But then, Betsy thought wryly to herself, it was unlikely that Lauren was going to post, "I think I'll be my completely self-centered self and stand up a work colleague for coffee this morning."

Betsy closed Facebook and opened WebMD. She searched on "dark skin spot," remembering the mark on her wrist she'd seen when writing on the chalkboard.

Is that mole skin cancer? WebMD asked back.

Oh, dear Lord. I have cancer, thought Betsy.

ELEVEN O'CLOCK

11:00 a.m.

At exactly eleven o'clock, a timer started to sound on one of James Brimmage's computers. *Ding ding ding ding.* James silenced it with the click of his mouse and put his work aside with satisfaction. As quickly as his bad mood had come on, it had now evaporated. Mary Beth's interruption hadn't actually affected his productivity for the hour, and he could now enjoy a well-earned rest.

For James, the eleven o'clock timer signaled the start of coffee hour. Some mornings he went to the faculty lounge. Other days he flirted with the baristas of Elm Grove. Either way, James preferred not to caffeinate alone. Today, James was in a quandary. He still hadn't settled the dilemma of whether to call Lauren Masters, his date from the evening before. *Should he suggest meeting for coffee?*

James's hand hovered briefly over the phone before he changed his mind and reached for the computer keyboard. A phone call indicated a level of commitment he wasn't interested in. He would email an off-hand coffee invitation to Lauren. If she showed for coffee, great. If not, he could move on with a clear conscience. He could even disguise his message as work related, so she didn't get the wrong idea. After all, he had to play the Lauren-card carefully. She was a colleague, a young professor, and took herself seriously.

He opened his email program and quickly typed his message.

> TO: *Lauren Masters*
> FROM: *James Brimmage*
> SUBJECT: *Help!*
> *Dear Lauren,*
> *I hope your today is as great as my yesterday was.*
> *I'm having some difficulty with my current research project and was hoping you had time to help me with it. I'll be at Wallaby's working on it between 11 and 12.*
> *I'll buy you a latte if you can solve my stochastic frontier model!*
> *James*

James pressed send and smiled to himself. Somewhat flirty with a soupçon of academic flattery. That should ease any morning-after tensions or regrets. Junior professors loved to feel intellectually indispensable by working out a problem for a fellow professor. To complete the ruse, James gathered together some notes and computer output from his research to bring to Wallaby's. He paused, however, when he noticed his email filter had highlighted an unread email from C.J. Whitmore in his inbox. Perhaps she'd changed her mind and wanted to meet up for coffee after all. If so, he could always ditch Lauren.

James clicked open C.J.'s message. A teaching award? For Betsy? James couldn't remember ever meeting anyone named Betsy since arriving at Eaton. However, he didn't like to burn any bridges that could lead to pleasure. He would endorse Betsy, and if she turned out to be young, gorgeous, and grateful, so much the better.

TO: Tenured Faculty
FROM: James Brimmage
SUBJECT: RE: Betsy Williams Teaching Award
G'day C.J.! I agree. We must support the teaching
staff. They are the backbone of the university. I would
be happy to write a letter of support for Betsy.
James

Ignoring the rest of his overfull inbox—responding to inane email was not something that improved James's enjoyment of life—James collected his research and headed out the door for his morning coffee. Wanting to stay out of the snow for as long as possible, James walked down to the basement floor of 42 Knollwood, cut through the Smythe Lounge, and headed towards the front of 40 Knollwood.

"Yoo hoo, Professor Brimmage!" Mary Beth called out as he passed her office.

James cursed under his breath and kept walking. Next time, he would brave the snow.

"Professor Brimmage! Over here!" Mary Beth was perched on the edge of her desk, her faux-crocodile-skin miniskirt dangerously high.

James believed in the market system—you always got what you paid for. A Porsche was a better car than a Kia. Housing was more expensive in New York City than Detroit. Filet mignon cost more than ground chuck.

Mary Beth Sanders was clearly the ground chuck of Elm Grove females. Moreover, she kept reappearing like a bad case of salmonella. Still walking, James tapped his left wrist in an exaggerated motion.

"G'day, Mary Beth," he said. "I'd love to chat, but I'm running late."

"But, Professor..." Mary Beth started.

"Got to go!" James said, as he disappeared out the

front door of 40 Knollwood. There was nothing Mary Beth could say that would increase his enjoyment of life.

11:05 a.m.

Walter looked out his office window and saw James Brimmage walking quickly away from the department. *Disposable good!* Walter thought instinctively, though he had no particular grudge against his colleague. Then, remembering the upcoming election, Walter changed his mind. No one was actually disposable today. He needed votes.

Departmental chair elections had a lively history in the Eaton Economics Department. Back in the nineteenth century, professors were hired and fired by a board of trustees, who also took it upon themselves to appoint the department chair. After tenure was introduced in the 1900s, the tenured faculty celebrated the arrival of democratic departmental elections by excluding their junior colleagues from participating. However, with the increasing focus on civil rights, even assistant professors were allowed to vote by 1965— though when that occurred each tenured professor was initially allowed two votes to make the transition more acceptable.

When the first elections were held, it had been expected that a candidate not vote for himself. That was the tradition in papal elections, and if it was good enough for God, it was good enough for Eaton. Initially, voters were placed on the honor system. However, after Professor Guillard cast a vote in the 1912 election and still won 9-0, a modified honor system was introduced. After 1912, voters were required to sign the back of their ballots, in case there was any issue. This system unraveled in the fateful election of 1947. The vote count for the two candidates, Professors Harvey and McDonald, indicated a 7-7 tie. To check the validity of the votes, the faculty inspected the signatures on the ballots. It turned out that Professor Harvey had voted for himself, with a poor forgery of Professor McDonald's signature on his ballot. Following that election, candidates were no longer allowed to vote at all. The honor system had no chance in the face of ambition.

The system of proxy voting in departmental elections—allowing a like-minded colleague to cast your vote while you enjoyed a long weekend—ended after the 1972 election between Professors Stevenson and Williams. Professor Blackman, a kingmaker for Professor Stevenson, had convinced three colleagues he was voting for Professor Williams. The colleagues had given Professor Blackman their proxy votes and had been startled to hear of the 11-0 victory for Professor Stevenson when they next came into work.

These days, the rules were simple. Both tenured and junior professors not running in the election were allowed one vote, and they had to cast their vote in person. Adjunct faculty were excluded from voting, of course. As were the candidates themselves. Participation in the election was voluntary, and a quorum had to be met for the election to be considered valid. The quorum had changed over the years—in light of the growth of the sabbatical—from 50% of the faculty down to five faculty members. And a simple majority ensured victory.

Walter thought about the upcoming vote. He went over to his office whiteboard, picked up a black marker, and drew a line down the middle. At the top of the left column, he wrote his own name in large capital letters.

At the top of the right column, he scribbled *Peter*.

Who was actually in at work today to vote? Well, clearly James Brimmage as Walter had just seen him. Could he count on James to vote for him? James seemed like the type to prefer strong leadership, and Peter could be so mousey and annoying. Walter wrote James's name in his own column but reluctantly added an asterisk. He needed to make sure James knew who the best candidate was.

The ever present Texan hussy would, of course, vote for Peter. What an ingrate. He'd tolerated her presence in the department with as much politeness and accommodation as she deserved. As soon as he was elected chair, he'd make her life so miserable that she'd gladly accept a teaching job at a high school. In the *Peter* column, Walter wrote down C.J.'s name.

What about lovely-legs Lauren? Walter paused, uncertain of her vote. She'd probably follow C.J.'s lead. Women went to the bathroom together, and so probably voted together too. Walter added Lauren's name to Peter's list, but put an asterisk by it. He'd turn on the charm and try to secure that vote.

Walter studied the whiteboard in front of him. Who else had he seen come into work today? It was snowy and the first day of the semester. Walter hadn't considered the problem before now, but he worried about the quorum. He thought back. C.J., Lauren, and James. Who else was there?

Arthur and Charles. Walter didn't understand why people that old were allowed to vote. It wasn't like they were going to live to see the consequences of their actions. However, given the quorum, he was glad they were at work today. Walter added Charles and Arthur to his side of the ledger. Life was about choice, and it was time Arthur and Charles knew they needed to choose him.

11:08 a.m.

"Betsy!" called out C.J. in her loud Texan twang. "Have you been waiting long?"

Betsy looked up and smiled. She hadn't seen C.J. since the end of the previous semester. With a husband, five children, and seventeen grandchildren, Betsy had spent most of the Christmas holidays shopping, cooking, decorating, sewing, knitting, and minding children. And she'd loved it. But she did miss her regular coffee breaks with her good friend.

"Give me two minutes to grab a coffee," C.J. said in a voice loud enough for Betsy to hear, as well as everyone else in Wallaby's coffee shop. C.J. grabbed a copy of the student newspaper, *The Pug Post,* and stood in line.

Betsy nodded her understanding and turned her attention back to her iPad. She perused the posted pictures of skin cancers and compared them to the mark on her wrist. It was definitely a melanoma. Dark in color, irregularly shaped. Or it could be a basal cell carcinoma. That was the most common form of cancer.

Betsy took a sip of her mocha whip latte. What had caused her to develop cancer? Should she be worrying about the amount of sugar in her diet? Or the amount of sleep she got? It was true that she'd been feeling tired by the end of her vacation. But she'd attributed that to the grandchildren. Betsy Googled *sugar and cancer.* Articles explaining why sugar was sweet poison, feeding cancer cells, stared back at her. *Oh, dear Lord,* thought Betsy. She pushed her mocha whip latte to one side.

Not wanting to read more about her impending sugar death, Betsy switched back to checking Facebook.

Today, several friends had *liked* a survey that told them what type of flower they resembled. The purpose of this activity wasn't clear to Betsy. Surely by now, in their old age, her friends all knew what flowers they liked or didn't like. But this survey claimed to channel their inner flower. Curious, Betsy clicked on the link.

> *"What are you at social gatherings?"*
>   A.   *The life of the party.*
>   B.   *A deep conversationalist.*
>   C.   *The quiet one in the corner.*

Betsy stared at the screen. What did this have to do with flowers? And there didn't seem to be an option D. *In the kitchen, cooking.*

"If you'd bothered to ask me, I'd have told you, you were a peony rose. Sweet and beautiful, and as pure as the day you were born," C.J. said, looking over Betsy's shoulder and reading the title of the quiz. "Now what in the world are you doing with one of those i-Fad doohickies?"

Betsy blushed and put the iPad away. "It's nothing. Just a Christmas gift. And I find Facebook useful. A way of keeping up with what the grandkids are doing. By the way, did you know sugar can kill you? It causes cancer."

"Uh huh. According to who? Some naturopath who failed high school statistics, no doubt. I wouldn't worry. If you want to read about death, read this."

C.J. put her copy of *The Pug Post* on the table in front of Betsy. The front page headline read *R.I.P.* in sixty-point font.

"Who died?" asked Betsy.

"Adorable Don." Adorable Don, the pug, was the mascot of Eaton University.

"That's terrible. How did he die?"

C.J. looked at the article. "It says here that he ate too much sugar."

Betsy looked worried.

"I'm joking. Old age, I think."

"What number was he?"

"Don the Twelfth, according to the article. I guess they're interviewing for Don the Thirteenth now."

"I wouldn't mind having a dog," Betsy mused. "The house is so empty now the holidays are over." Betsy looked at the mark on her wrist, uncertainly. "Of course, I'd have to be around to look after it."

C.J. followed Betsy's gaze. "Betsy, dearest, I'm detecting some Google-induced hypochondria. Are you accusing that innocent mole of being skin cancer? It's an ordinary, harmless mole. Now, I suggest you stop Googling your way to an early grave, enjoy your coffee, and chat with me. A real person. Search engines and social media are highly overrated."

Chagrined, Betsy drank some of her mocha latte. "It is good to see you," Betsy acknowledged. "How's your first day of semester?"

"Frustrating. I'm trying to cajole the new faculty into agreeing to present a seminar. James Brimmage and Arthur Fleitman have said yes. But no luck yet with Lauren Masters. She had the audacity to tell me she was too busy to talk, when the woman was clearly doing her morning crossword."

"She must really like her crossword. She actually posted a picture of it on Facebook this morning, with the caption 'Solving the problem of getting tenure.'"

C.J. made a face. "That woman is a walking disaster of affirmative action. How else can you explain why someone with that little intelligence or ability got hired at Eaton?"

Betsy sighed. "Perhaps she has qualities that just haven't become apparent to us yet."

"Betsy. You are an Eaton-trained economist. Apply the principle of Occam's razor—the simplest explanation is the best. I can explain Lauren Masters' presence in the department a couple of ways. One: her appointment was a clerical error. Or two: in spite of the evidence, the woman's an intellectual giant; Peter Johansson saw this talent when he hired her; and, for the first time in Eaton history, the Economics Department thought it would be terrific to have another female faculty member. I don't know about you, but option one seems reasonable. Option two does not."

C.J. took a long, defiant sip of her sugar-filled coffee.

"Well," said Betsy, "regardless of how she got here, I think we should still be welcoming. You know, woman to woman."

"But there's something about her I really don't like."

"Can you be more specific?"

"I wish I could. It's just a feeling. Lauren is just a little too...confident? I'm not even sure if that's the word I mean."

"Peter Johansson was just here, waiting to meet her, and she didn't show. I thought at the time she was just being rude, but she might be a little overwhelmed, you know. Maybe she's pretending to be confident, to cover up her insecurity."

"That's possible, but not very probable. Come to lunch today at twelve. I'm meeting her at Antonio's. Apparently it's the only time she had free in her busy schedule. I'm surprised she didn't post it on Facebook already."

11:10 a.m.

Arthur Fleitman was startled awake midway through a rumbling, snuffling snore. A long string of drool hung from his mouth, and his slack jaw gave him a remarkable resemblance to a stroke victim. He lay back in his La-Z-Boy recliner, blinking at the ceiling. His copy of the *Yachting Times* lay on the floor, unread.

Arthur looked over at his wall clock and took note of the time. Ten minutes past eleven. *Darn*, he thought. *Why had he woken from his morning nap so early?* He still had to occupy fifty minutes until lunch at twelve. Arthur closed his eyes and tried to fall back to sleep.

Someone knocked loudly on his office door. The knock sounded angry and impatient. As if the person had already knocked once and was offended at being ignored.

"Go away!" Arthur yelled.

"Thanks for the kind welcome," said Walter Scovill, as he stepped into Arthur's office. "Not too busy, I hope?" Walter raised an expressive eyebrow in the direction of the La-Z-Boy. Walter wasn't surprised to find his former Ph.D. supervisor resting. According to the gossip from Princeton, the man had napped through most of the last decade.

Arthur exhaled with frustration. There were many things Arthur disliked about college life. High on the list were schmoozing with the Dean, pretentious dinners with old men wearing mortarboards, and emails informing him of exciting new teaching technologies to enhance the online learning experience. But having his day incessantly disturbed by colleagues popping through the door like Whack-a-Moles was particularly distasteful. *You hit one back and another one pops up.*

"Is there some reason in particular that you dropped by, Walt?" he asked. "Or did you just want to shoot the breeze?"

Walter sneered a smile. "Always good to see you,

Art. So glad you decided to spend your best years here at Eaton. I won't waste your valuable time with small talk."

Arthur closed his eyes again. With any luck, he'd fall asleep and miss whatever unimportant diatribe Walter was about to embark on. Walter Scovill had been a snot of a graduate student, and age hadn't improved the man.

Walter cleared his throat. "Ahem. Arthur?"

Reluctantly, Arthur opened his eyes again. "I thought you weren't going to waste my time. What is it you want to say?"

Walter sat down in the wooden chair that Arthur kept for visitors, unsurprised by the discomfort. Years ago, Arthur had admitted that he made sure his visitors' chair was as uncomfortable as possible, to discourage any thoughts of a lengthy office chat. "Well, yes. As you know, the vote for chair of the department is this afternoon."

Arthur, his eyes closed again, snorted loudly.

Walter looked down at Arthur, unsure if the older man had snored in his sleep, or snorted in derision. "Arthur?" he asked, uncertainly.

Arthur opened his eyes.

"What?"

"Well, I wanted to make sure I could count on your vote this afternoon," Walter said. "I, of course, will work for your needs when I am chair." Walter left it unsaid, but understood, that if Arthur didn't vote for him and Walter became chair, he'd do everything in his power to make Arthur's life a living hell.

Arthur snorted again, and then actually laughed out loud. He reached down and moved the lever of the La-Z-Boy, so the chair rotated to the upright position. Sitting up, Arthur looked Walter directly in the eye. "You don't intimidate me. I'm too old and too ugly to care about anything you think you could do."

"Intimidation?" said Walter, feigning hurt feelings. "I thought we knew each other better than that. Surely there's something you want...a lighter teaching load perhaps? I could guarantee you would teach one fewer classes a year, if I became chair."

"That is tempting," said Arthur. "I do hate teaching, especially undergraduate classes."

"Well, then," said Walter. "I think we understand each other." He stood up and started to walk towards the door.

"Of course," added Arthur, "Peter also understands that I don't like teaching."

Walter turned back to face his former professor. "I doubt Peter understands your needs as well as I do."

"Really? It was his understanding that I needed to reduce my class load by two classes a year." Arthur smiled as he lied to Walter. Peter had never come by to talk about the election, and Arthur hadn't sought him out.

Walter spat out his reply. "Two classes a year and an extra TA. Take it or leave it."

"How generous of you, Walt," said Arthur, as he levered his La-Z-Boy back to the reclining position, signaling Walter's dismissal.

"But," called out Arthur, as Walter was leaving the room, "I may be tempted to vote for Charles."

Walter spun around. "What? What are you talking about? Charles who?"

"Charles Covington III. He let me know that he's intending to throw his hat in the ring. The experienced candidate. It has some appeal to an old guy like me."

11:12 a.m.

Mary Beth was settled in her office, getting ready to soothe her ruffled feelings with another episode of *Say Yes to the Dress*. It had been a difficult morning of assisting. First, the lady from human resources had been so rude. Then, Mary Beth had trekked all the way across the road in the snow to talk to Lauren Masters, and she hadn't even been in her office. Even Professor Brimmage, her future husband, was being a grumpy-bumpy. Why hadn't he stopped to chat? As for Professor Flightman, well...Mary Beth just shook her head. The man might be smart, but he hadn't learned any manners.

Mary Beth, leaning forward to open her Netflix account, caught sight of the copy job she still needed to do for Lauren Masters. It was, like, totally not cool that Lauren-Long-Legs was making her feel so guilty about this photocopying. Not that Lauren had actually said anything yet that morning. But Mary Beth knew she would. Her type always did. And in such a catty way. Like, "Oh. That photocopying isn't done yet? Well, I guess I'll just have to do it myself." Or "Well, if you can get it done by the end of the week, that would be great," when it was so obvious they didn't think it was great and they were going to bitch about you in the faculty lounge for the rest of the week.

It wasn't as if Mary Beth could just drop everything and do it right now. She was legally obliged to take a fifteen minute break every morning, so as not to get that repetitive wrist strain thingy. And she was already late for her break this morning. It was after eleven and she needed her rest. The law said so.

As the first *Say Yes* bride-to-be confessed she couldn't afford to spend more than $2000 on a dress (a figure so low it caused Mary Beth to scoff), Walter Scovill stormed into her office.

"Where is Charles Covington?" he demanded.

Mary Beth paused her show. "I'm on break at the moment, Professor Scovill. Can you come back in fifteen?"

Walter snarled, and Mary Beth decided she could delay the remainder of her break. She looked around the office, trying to be helpful. "Professor Covington's not here, Professor Scovill."

"I didn't ask where he wasn't. I want to know where he is."

Mary Beth nodded. "Well, I'd look somewhere else then. Have you tried his office?"

"Do I look like a man who has time to wander aimlessly around the campus, looking for colleagues?"

"Um, no. I guess not," Mary Beth lied. In her opinion, if anyone had time to waste it was the professors. She had to assist eight hours a day, five days a week, fifty weeks a year. They only taught classes for a few hours a week, and the semester was only fifteen weeks long.

"So..."

"It's after eleven. Most people have a morning coffee about now. You could try the faculty lounge." Mary Beth pasted on a smile.

"Here's an idea. Why don't you find Charles, and when you do, let him know I want to see him. At once!"

Walter left the office before Mary Beth could placate him with a another lie. *Sure thing. I'll get right on that*, she thought, as she resumed watching her show.

11:20 a.m.

James Brimmage charmed his way into Wallaby's coffee shop. He smiled at a sleepy-eyed, sweatpants-wearing co-ed, who then giggled coquettishly as she left through the door James held open for her. He showed a coy dimple to the attractive, older woman in line ahead of him waiting for coffee, and was rewarded with a phone number. And he flirted shamelessly with the barista making his cappuccino.

"G'day, mate. I think I feel extra foamy this morning," James said with a wink.

The barista, a hardened young woman who worked long hours serving entitled Eatonians in order to pay her own way through the local state college, smiled despite herself. There was something irresistible about James's Australian accent, good looks, and love of life.

Betsy and C.J. watched the carnage of young women fall in James's wake.

"I'd love to know that man's testosterone level," commented C.J. "It must be three standard deviations above the national average."

"It's certainly higher than Mr. Williams's," Betsy said.

C.J. laughed. "I won't tell." The two women watched James accept another phone number as he added sugar and cream to his coffee.

"The man is an anthropological paper, just waiting to be written up," said C.J. "Or maybe it's me. Am I the only woman in Elm Grove who can resist him?"

Betsy smiled. "I'm pretty sure I can withstand his charms, as well."

"Well, we're about to put that to the test. Don Juan is approaching. Brace yourself."

James—coffee in one hand and research papers in the other—had looked around for Lauren Masters and noticed both her absence and C.J.'s presence. Happy with the switch, he walked over to C.J. and Betsy, oozing conviviality and good humor.

"Hello, James. Would you like to join us for coffee?" asked C.J. She was amazed that the man showed no reticence or embarrassment, given their interaction earlier that morning.

"I'd love to join you ladies," said James. "I was going to meet Lauren Masters and chat with her about some research," James waved his folder of papers as evidence of this claim. "But it seems I've been stood-up."

"Well, take a seat and enjoy your coffee," said C.J. "Betsy and I are meeting Lauren for lunch at Antonio's at twelve. Come along, and we can all hash out your research question. Are you free?"

James gave both women his award-winning smile. "As a bird. That sounds wonderful."

"And don't feel bad about Lauren," added Betsy. "She missed her coffee date with Peter Johansson as well."

"How interesting. In that case, I won't take it personally," said James. "I'm James, by the way." James held out his hand to Betsy, who gave him a wry smile as she shook his hand.

"I know," she said. "We met at the end of last semester, when you joined the department. I'm Betsy Williams, an instructor in the Econ Department."

"Betsy?" he echoed. "The one getting the teaching award?"

"No. You must be thinking of another Betsy. I'm not getting a teachng award."

"Yes," C.J. interrupted quickly. "I think you're confused, James." She gave James a long, meaningful look.

James laughed inwardly. *This was clearly the Betsy of C.J.'s email. And equally clearly, C.J. hadn't mentioned the teaching award to her yet.* He winked at C.J., to show her he understood.

"My mistake," he said gallantly. He picked up C.J.'s copy of *The Pug Post*, in an attempt to change the subject. "Who died?" asked James, looking at the front page headline.

11:39 a.m.

If Charles Covington III was being perfectly honest with himself, Arthur Fleishman's enthusiasm for Charles's run for office has unnerved the older man. After their conversation, Charles had returned to his office to rehydrate. *Just a nip, to take the edge off the old nerves*, he assured himself, as he poured out a healthy tumblerful of gin from his reserve bottle.

Given their similar ages, Charles had expected Arthur to compliment him on his wisdom and experience. He even thought that Arthur might give him a pat on the back for contemplating a run. But ultimately, Charles had expected to be talked out of the idea. *Seizing the day* was all very well, but it also took a great deal of energy. Energy he no longer had. *Was he really expected to run for department chair now? Against Walter Scovill? What if he won?*

Charles took another sizable sip from the tumbler. On the upside, thinking about Walter Scovill had made his problems with Mildred seem benign. She was a wonderful wife.

Charles wondered if he could gracefully back out of the plan, now that he'd announced it to Arthur. Perhaps he should talk to the younger voters and see if there was general interest in his candidacy. There was no point in running if he was only going to receive Arthur's vote. Surely Arthur would understand that. But, Charles conceded, if the entire department really wanted him as their leader, he wouldn't turn away from his duty.

He looked at his wall clock. Whatever was going to happen, it needed to happen soon. It was after eleven on the morning of the election. *No time like the present to search for the truth,* as his therapist liked to say.

Charles hooked his fingers under his red suspenders and headed out the door.

A few minutes later, Charles knocked on Lauren Masters' door. "Lauren?" he called out. "You in there?" Charles knocked again on her door and tried to turn the handle. The door was locked.

"I wish I was allowed to start my work day in the afternoon," complained a voice behind him. Charles turned around and saw Mary Beth.

After watching two episodes of *Say Yes,* Mary Beth had decided attack was the best form of defense when it came to someone like Lauren Masters. She'd returned to Lauren's office to try, yet again, to tell her about the training that afternoon. That way, if Lauren had any complaints about missing the training or her photocopying not being done, Mary Beth could truthfully let her know that she'd spent the entire morning chasing after Lauren. That should shut her up.

"Hello, again," said Charles. He was pleased to see that Mary Beth wasn't crying anymore. "Are you looking for Lauren as well?"

"Yeah, but I don't know why I bother. She's, like, on my case to get some work done for her. And the human resources lady is on my case to talk to Lauren. But I don't think she's even come into work yet today. Are you sure you saw her earlier?"

"The human resources lady?" asked Charles, not following Mary Beth's train of thought.

"No, not her. Lauren. When we were talking in 40 Knollwood, you said you'd seen Lauren this morning. Are you sure you saw her?"

Charles nodded, finally understanding Mary Beth's question. "I definitely saw Lauren this morning. She was walking into work at the same time I was."

"Well, I'm, like, supposed to tell her about this diversity training thing this afternoon. But if she can't stay in her office, I can't help her. You saw me here, right? If she calls again, mad at me, I'm going to tell her to call you, and you can let her know that I tried to to tell Lauren. Okay?"

"Indeed," agreed Charles, not at all sure about who was going to call, or what he was supposed to say. He headed for the front door of 43 Knollwood in an attempt to extract himself from the confusion of Mary Beth.

"Oh, Professor Covington, I almost forgot."

Charles turned back.

"I'm supposed to tell you that Professor Scovill wants to see you."

"Well, you can tell him that I'm going to the faculty lounge and he can find me there."

"But he wants you to find him."

"Why would I do that? I don't want to see him."

11:47 a.m.

The faculty lounge for the Eaton Economics Department was best described as a mid-nineteenth-century man-cave. Unlike the Smythe Lounge, which was a glorified thoroughfare, the faculty lounge was secluded and private. It was filled with old leather chairs, whiskey tumblers, and hunting prints. Moreover, it seemed the new-fangled Eaton University non-smoking policy didn't apply within, judging by the cigar ends and pipe remnants that littered the room.

The lounge was located in 42 Knollwood and was a regular hangout for faculty looking to fill in time between pesky teaching obligations or delay the onerous duties of graduate student supervision. As today was the first day of the semester, the faculty

lounge was notably empty, as the majority of the
professors at Eaton viewed the first week of semester as
an unofficial extension of their vacation. Flex time, as it
were. After all, they were so brilliant they could teach
the fifteen-week syllabus in fourteen weeks. Or even
thirteen, if needed.

At present, the only person in the faculty lounge was
Peter Johansson. He'd stopped in, hoping to canvass
more votes for the election. However, seeing the room
empty and *The New York Times* lying untouched on one
of the coffee tables, Peter suspended his campaign for a
momentary coffee and crossword puzzle break. He'd
just nestled deep into his favorite leather armchair, feet
up on an ottoman, and was chuckling over the clue
Demanding subj. when Charles Covington III stumbled
into the room.

"Hello, Peter," said Charles, as he made his way
over to the coffee pot.

Peter nodded, thinking that coffee was a good idea
for Charles. The aroma of gin was strong this morning.

Charles, coffee cup in hand, began to mumble to
himself. "Non-fat, one-percent, two-percent...non-fat
again?"

"Problem, Charles?" asked Peter, looking up from
his puzzle.

"What's with the diet milk? I want half-and-half in
my coffee. *Carpe diem*, if you know what I mean. No
point in drinking colored water."

Peter, who only drank non-fat milk in an effort to
protect his heart, nodded sympathetically. "I'm sure it
was just an oversight. But you know what, Charles?
The vote for chair of the department is this afternoon. If
I become chair, I promise you that there will always be
half-and-half for your coffee." Peter smiled. He figured
Charles was so soused that this would seem reasonable
to him.

"Great! Wait…no."

"Is there a problem?" asked Peter.

"Actually, yes. I had the idea this morning of running for the chair position myself. The voice of experience, and all that. I told Arthur Fleitman, and he thought it was a good idea. But now I'm not so sure."

Peter stared at Charles. Surely he hadn't heard right. The old fellow was running for chair? Peter couldn't figure out if this would work in his favor or not. It would cost him Charles's vote for sure—if Charles was running, he couldn't vote. And Charles would never have voted for Walter. But would Charles attract other voters who would otherwise have voted for Walter? Better to play it safe, and make sure Charles didn't cost him the election.

"I agree with Arthur. It's a great idea, taking a stand for experience. The department needs someone like you. But it's pretty late in the game to start your campaign. Would you think about joining my ticket as a vice chair, and bringing all the wisdom of your experience to my campaign?"

Vice chair? thought Charles. He hadn't heard of such a position. However, the idea was appealing—vice chair would certainly be less responsibility, but not without influence. What was his wife, Mildred, always saying? *It's the neck that turns the head.* As vice chair, he could still bring common sense and experience to departmental decisions. Certainly, he had more chance as vice chair than as a defeated candidate. And then, there were all those vice Presidents in history that went on to become President. Perhaps he needed to think of the long game. If he changed his mind, and wanted the chair position in a few years, this would increase the probability that it could be his.

Charles cleared his throat. "Well, that's a sound point."

"Good," agreed Peter, marveling at his new-found political acumen. "Let's have lunch at Antonio's today and discuss strategy. Say, noon?"

Charles was just starting to agree, when Arthur Fleitman ambled into the room. Having had his morning nap disturbed to the point where sleep now proved unobtainable, Arthur had decided to occupy the time remaining until lunch with coffee and the paper. He was disappointed to see that he wasn't alone in this thought. He disliked socializing, especially while reading *The New York Times*. Other people, especially opinionated ones, infringed upon his favorite past-time of criticizing the government. Arthur knew that if he was in charge of the world, it would be a much better place. But he also knew that he didn't care enough about the world to exert the effort required to run it. So all that was left was to enjoy moaning about the poor job the fools currently in power were doing.

Arthur poured himself a cup of coffee and sniffed at the contents in his cup. *Burnt.* Arthur hated burnt coffee. Discontentedly, he added two-percent milk, three packets of white sugar, and stirred. Hopefully the sugar would disguise the burned taste. It wasn't as if he was going to make fresh coffee himself. What was he? A secretary? Arthur, sipping half-heartedly at his drink, turned and faced Charles and Peter.

"Well, it looks as if we have two-thirds of the candidates here. Almost enough for one of those ghastly presidential-style debates that have become so popular with the uninformed masses. Should I moderate while you gentleman hash out the issues of the day?"

"Ah, yes. Well, there's been a slight change in plans," said Charles. "I'm now running on the same ticket as Peter, as his vice chair. I hope we can still count on your vote. Come to lunch with Peter and myself at Antonio's at twelve. I'll tell you all about it."

"Sounds interesting," Arthur lied. It seemed the amusement value of the election had fallen markedly, given this new development. "Peter, would you mind tossing me the front section of the *Times*. I need to see what disastrous policies our beloved government has concocted in the last twenty-four hours."

Peter handed the paper to Arthur. "So, can we count on your vote, Arthur?" Peter pushed.

"Can you believe these ninnies?" asked Arthur, rhetorically, as he read the day's headlines. "Peace in the Middle East. Who are they kidding?"

"Can we count on your vote this afternoon?" asked Peter, more insistently.

Arthur looked up. "Well, I'd love to vote for you and Charles, but my teaching load is so heavy these days. I don't think I'll have time."

"Teaching load, did you say?" asked Charles. "I was thinking we should have the junior faculty take on more of that sort of thing."

Peter raised an eyebrow. "Perhaps no teaching once a faculty member is aged over, say, seventy?"

"That sounds about right," agreed Arthur. "If you need to justify it, argue it's best for the students. The younger professors have been trained more recently, and their knowledge is more cutting edge…"

Arthur's justification was cut short as the door to the faculty lounge slammed open, and Walter Scovill blustered inside. He'd tired of waiting around for Charles and had started his own search for him. He pointed a finger at Charles. "What's this I hear? Are you running for chair this afternoon? Don't embarrass yourself, you…"

Arthur deftly cut off Walter's diatribe. "I'm so glad you're here, Walt. Peter was just asking me about my vote for this afternoon. You don't know the latest, but Charles and Peter have combined forces. Peter's campaigning with Charles as his running mate. I believe the new position is being called vice chair."

"Vice chair?" sputtered Walter, not yet comprehending.

"That's right, vice chair. They were just explaining their campaign policy of removing the teaching requirement for faculty aged over seventy. I think it'll be quite attractive to the geriatric demographic."

"No teaching at all?" repeated Walter. "Well, I can match that. And I'll throw in a pair of graduate students as well."

Peter sucked in his breath. "Now, Walter, surely you learned from last semester. The graduate students aren't actually our property to barter and use as we please."

"What else are they good for?"

"Well," said Arthur, who was now enjoying the pre-election entertainment immensely, "I don't think I find the offer of graduate labor appealing. It seems rather colonial, don't you think?"

Walter rolled his eyes. Arthur Fleitman had never blinked twice at graduate labor before today. In fact, Arthur had happily treated Walter like a piece of chattel during Walter's graduate school years.

"I think, realistically, Peter and Charles have sown up the elderly vote, Walter," Arthur continued. "Perhaps you should think about the female demographic? You could choose a female running mate. A tip of the cap to Sarah Palin, or Hillary Clinton if she's more your style. Of course, that only leaves you C.J. or Lauren as options. If you want my opinion, Lauren looks to be the more malleable of the two."

"I don't want your opinion," said Walter. "And I don't want a running mate. And if I did, I certainly wouldn't choose a woman. It's bad enough I have to go home to my wife every night."

"I don't know if you're thinking rationally at the

moment, Walter."

Walter bridled. He prided himself on his rationality. It was the quality that made him superior to everyone else on the planet.

"Really? I can't wait to hear this. Explain why it would be rational for me to choose a running mate."

"I think for the same reason the presidential candidates do," observed Arthur dryly. "To boost their vote totals."

Walter smiled. "Art, you clearly don't have all the facts. Faculty members running for election at Eaton can't vote for themselves. If Peter and I have vice chairs, that will be four people excluded from the election. I doubt we'll even reach quorum."

"Wait a minute," Peter interjected. "Where in the rules does it say the vice chairs can't vote? There isn't even an official position called vice chair."

"There isn't?" asked Charles, confused.

"Sorry to burst your bubble, Walter. But the vice chair is merely an endorsement," continued Peter. "We're only voting for the position of chair. Therefore, only the chair candidates are excluded from voting."

"Who are you kidding?" sneered Walter. "If you want Charles as your vice chair, he can't vote."

"Says who?" asked Peter. "I'm acting chair at the moment, and I say the vice chairs can vote."

"Let's not fight," said Arthur, who was thoroughly enjoying the spat. "Apparently, we are all going to lunch at Antonio's in a few minutes. Put on your happy face, Walt, come with us, and you can decide on your running mate over a plate of over-priced pasta."

TWELVE NOON

12:00 p.m.

The population of Elm Grove was less than one hundred thousand, even when the students were in town. Consequently, the multiplex only had eight screens, the Walmart was a neighborhood market instead of a supercenter, and there was only one decent restaurant within walking distance of the Economics Department.

Antonio's Trattoria was many things, but it definitely was not a trattoria. It was a quiet Italian restaurant with white tablecloths, professional waiters, and a notoriously expensive wine list. The lunch trade at Antonio's was comprised almost exclusively of faculty from the Economics Department, the business school, and the law school, with an occasional Eaton administrator for variety. They were the only people in Elm Grove with both the time and money to consider a $45 steak a reasonable option for their midday meal. Everyone else in town had to slum it at the plastic-spork eateries scattered around the college, eating the soup and half sandwich combo meal while perched at an easy-to-clean laminate table top.

C.J. and Betsy walked the five-minute distance from Wallaby's to Antonio's, bundled up against the snow.

"I'm going to take my next sabbatical in Tahiti," C.J. said, as she negotiated the icy sidewalk in her hot pink cowboy boots. "Just me, the beach, and a mojito. Doesn't that sound perfect?"

Betsy, who was wearing a long, black, imitation-down-filled coat, sensible winter boots, and a bright blue woolen hat with ear flaps, was not feeling the cold. However, she still agreed with C.J. that Elm Grove was gray from November to April. The beach, and some sunshine, would be nice. "I'll come visit," she offered.

"Well, it'll only happen if Peter wins the election for chair this afternoon. Walter Scovill will do anything and everything to make my life miserable if he gets elected, including denying my sabbatical request."

"Can he do that?" asked Betsy.

"Absolutely. The department chair has to approve all leave applications. Most chairs just rubber stamp a sabbatical request. But Walter loves to use the power. For someone like Walter, power is as essential as food and water. I'm sure he's desperate to win."

"Do you really think Walter has a chance to win the election?" Betsy asked. "My impression was that Peter had been doing a good job."

"I'd agree with that. Peter's been pretty good. Not spectacular, of course. But no one expected him to be spectacular. The problem is the election is being held today. It's the first day of the semester, and it's snowing."

"Why is the election today? It doesn't seem that smart to hold it on the first day of the semester."

"No idea, but I think it's always held on the first day of the semester. You should ask Charles. He knows all the historical reasons for strange department traditions."

"Maybe, in years past, all the professors showed up for the first day of class."

"Times change, that's for sure. It's possible the only people who turn up to vote today are the ardent Walter supporters. Peter doesn't exactly inspire electoral passion."

"Who in the department is a Walter supporter? Are

there any?"

"I don't know. Arthur Fleitman, maybe? For some reason, he reminds me of an older, more bitter version of Walter."

"Is there anything you can do to rally support for Peter? Maybe you can convince the ardent Walter haters to vote."

"I was thinking we should chat with Lauren and James over lunch. They're both new. It's possible they haven't seen enough of Walter yet to realize what a horse's patootie he is." C.J. paused, thinking. "Though, it seems they've seen enough of each other in the short time they've been at Eaton."

"What do you mean?"

"Exactly what you think I mean. Clearly, those two are sleeping together."

"James and Lauren? Really?"

"Of course. The man came to Wallaby's looking for…Lauren. He didn't walk directly over to lunch with us, but offered to go via the department to walk with…Lauren. The man can't help but flirt with women, and the most attractive woman we all know is…"

"Lauren," Betsy finished. "I hadn't thought of that, but she did post something on her Facebook page about meeting up with an old friend. Do you think she and James knew each other before they joined the department at Eaton?"

"It's possible. Academia is a small, incestuous world." C.J. sighed as she thought about the upcoming lunch at Antonio's with the departmental lovebirds. "I hate eating lunch out. It's such a time-suck."

Betsy nodded, though it wasn't the amount of time lunch was going to consume that worried her. It was the cost. Because of Betsy's adjunct-instructor salary, she'd never been to Antonio's. In fact, she didn't eat lunch at any restaurants, fancy or otherwise. Instead, she brought a brown bag to work every day. Today, she'd packed a very sensible turkey and lettuce sandwich, an apple, and some Oreo cookies for an afternoon pick-me-up. *Surely Antonio's serves an inexpensive, garden salad*, reasoned Betsy to herself. *That would be perfect.* After all, she should be dieting. Her iPad had told her so.

"Lauren Masters really knows how to push my buttons," C.J. continued. "She'd better agree to give a seminar, after all this."

12:07 p.m.

"Can I get you started with something to drink?" asked the disdainful waiter, who'd introduced himself as Timothy, while raising an expressive eyebrow at C.J.'s choice of footwear and Betsy's blue hat. Years of experience had taught him that people in colorful clothes never tipped well.

"We're actually waiting for two more people, Timothy," said C.J. "So we'll hold off on ordering."

"Some sparkling water, perhaps," suggested Timothy.

"Perhaps not," replied C.J.

Timothy hovered near the table, ready to take their order and move them along, so space could be made for the more generous tippers. C.J. pointedly turned to Betsy. "How did your classes go this morning?" she asked.

"Good, I think. By the way, what was that teaching award that James mentioned?"

"I don't know," C.J. lied. "I hate the first day of class. It's like starting a conversation with a stranger at a dinner party—awkward."

"I broke the ice by asking the students to define economics. They seem to think it's about making money."

"Did you direct them to the business school?"

"No. I think they'll find their own way there."

"Well, if you have any problem students, you can send them to Mary Beth."

"Mary Beth Sanders?"

"Yes, and don't look so shocked. I'm just joking. The woman showed me her manicure this morning—a ghastly green job with mortar boards—and she thinks it will inspire the students."

"Inspire them? To do what?"

"God only knows. I can't comprehend how that woman's mind works. I've met gerbils that are smarter than her."

Before Betsy could reply, Timothy returned. "Are you still waiting for your dining companions?"

C.J. pointed to the two empty chairs at the four-top table. "Does it look like our dining companions have arrived?" she asked.

Timothy shook his head.

"Then I guess we're still waiting," said C.J.

"Do you know what you get when you mix stupidity with insolence?" C.J. asked Betsy, while she looked meaningfully at Timothy.

"He's not so bad," Betsy defended. "He's just trying to do his job."

"You're too nice. I wonder what's taking James and Lauren so long. Or perhaps I don't want to know."

"It's the middle of the day," objected Betsy. "Surely not."

"You'd be horrified if you knew everything that happened behind the closed doors in the Economics Department in the middle of the day. Well, I don't think Timothy will let us wait around forever. I'm going to check out the menu."

C.J. opened the large, leather-covered menu in front of her, looked over the options, and then decisively closed it. Betsy glanced at her menu uncertainly.

Timothy approached them again. "Ready to order?"

C.J. looked over at Betsy, whose face was furrowed with indecision. "Nope, not ready yet. But thanks for checking, Timmy."

While waiting for Betsy to decide on her lunch, C.J. looked around the room. Antonio's hadn't succumbed to the new industrial-look trend in restaurants. You couldn't see into the kitchen. There were no exposed wooden beams across the ceiling. There was a conspicuous absence of concrete and steel in the decor. Instead, the chairs were plush and comfortable, the floor was carpeted, and the ceiling was low. In one corner of the room, a wood-burning fireplace crackled. *If it wasn't for the people, it would be a delightful place to eat lunch.*

"Having trouble deciding?" asked C.J., when she realized that Betsy was still studying the menu.

"Well, there are so many choices," lied Betsy. Actually, the problem was that there weren't any choices. Everything on the menu was well over Betsy's budget, and she wasn't sure what most of it was. *A duo of beef?* Surely they weren't going to serve two cows. *White truffle madeira emulsion?* Betsy had thought that an emulsion was a type of paint. And the garden salad was actually a "medley of organic arugula, watercress, frisée, mizuna, mache, and tatsoi with accents of candied pecans, roasted beets, and red Anjou pears."

"I know," agreed C.J. "You'd think more choice would be better. But actually, it's just as bad as not enough choice. With too many choices, you start drowning in the options." C.J. paused. "Maybe that's why Peter hired Lauren. He was overwhelmed by the number of choices."

"I think more choice is better," said Betsy.

"Could be. But I find it helpful to reduce my choices. Like now—I randomly picked out three things on the menu, and chose from those three. You should try it."

"What did you choose?"

"Duo of beef, cooked rare, hold the vegetables. Don't want to confuse the poor beasts and have them think they're still grazing there on the plate.

"And Betsy," C.J. added, as if as an afterthought, "I hope you won't fight me on this, but as I asked you to lunch, I insist on treating. It's a Texas thing. My daddy'd skin me alive if he knew I hadn't been a proper host."

Betsy smiled her thanks, and was back perusing the menu—the entire menu—when C.J. muttered something under her breath that sounded like "pluck a duck." Betsy looked up to see Walter, Arthur, Peter, and Charles standing next to the *maitre'd*, waiting to be seated.

12:12 p.m.

Walter Scovill, standing with his colleagues in the entrance of Antonio's Restaurant, was debating whether he should grab a fork off the closest table and ram it through his eye, or if he should excuse himself to the men's room and snort cocaine. The walk over to the restaurant had been interminable. It had taken them ten minutes to leave the Economics Department, as Arthur needed his coat, Peter had to pick up his wallet from his office, and Charles needed to change his hearing aid batteries. Then Walter had been stuck talking to Charles Covington III on the walk over to the restaurant. Did the man really think Walter was interested in his marital difficulties? Mildred's new-found independence was of even less importance to Walter than his students' education.

Walter was eyeing the nearby silverware when Charles called out to a table across the restaurant, "C.J.! Betsy! What a surprise! Having lunch as well? I hope you'll join us."

Walter looked up to see C.J. Whitmore and her fat friend getting up from their chairs, and a waiter helpfully pushing another table up to theirs.

"Splendid. Splendid," said Charles, as he walked over to the newly-formed large lunch table. "This is a treat, to have lunch with such lovely ladies." C.J. rolled her eyes, but Betsy smiled back at Charles. They'd known each other since Betsy was a graduate student half a century ago. There was always comfort in the company of such a familiar person.

Walter shuddered. *Dante had been wrong,* he thought to himself. *There was actually a tenth circle of hell, and it appeared he was in it. If the election wasn't that afternoon, he would walk out of the restaurant without saying a word.*

Arthur stood off to the side, scowling. He hated eating at pretentious restaurants like Antonio's. He hated menus that called beans "haricots vert" or egg whites "sea foam," and he especially hated being served food higher than it was wide.

C.J., realizing the expanded lunch party was inevitable, counted chairs. The joined tables now seated six. "We still need two more places," she said to Timothy. "James and Lauren are coming," she mentioned to the men who'd joined her lunch, uninvited.

A much happier and more helpful Timothy returned with two chairs. A table of eight always resulted in an extravagant tip, especially if they started drinking.

Timothy squeezed the last two chairs at the corners of one table, and everyone began to sit down. Walter made himself the head of one table. Arthur was the head of the other. C.J. and Peter sat on either side of Arthur and Betsy sat next to C.J. and, unfortunately, Walter. Charles took the remaining seat across from Betsy.

Timothy reappeared with wine lists, lunch menus, and a list of daily specials that he hadn't bothered to give Betsy and C.J. when they'd initially sat down. As the menus were passed around, Walter turned to Peter. "Well, as you're still acting chair of the department for the next two hours, I believe you have the power to pay for this lunch. It is, of course, up to you. But if I were chair, I'd cover the expense. I'm sure we'll talk important departmental business. But I understand that you've made a point to be more frugal with the department's money in my absence."

Everyone looked at Peter. Lunch would be much more enjoyable, not to mention extravagant and sumptuous, if they knew the department was picking up the tab. Peter looked uncomfortable. This was a great opportunity to campaign for votes. But Walter was right. Part of Peter's campaign was that he was the fiscally responsible candidate. A policy that wasn't going to win any favors right now.

"Well, I suppose...one lunch wouldn't hurt anyone..." Peter faltered.

The menus at the table opened with enthusiasm. While those present at the table didn't like everyone (or, in some cases, anyone) they were eating lunch with, they all loved free food. Ever Arthur.

Timothy, sensing the mood at the table, appeared smiling. "Can I get you any drinks today?"

Walter, aiming to both spend the department's money and reduce the unpleasantness of the meal, ordered a double scotch straight up. "And keep them coming," he told Timothy.

Timothy was bringing out the first of the drinks when James Brimmage walked in. "G'day all. I didn't realize this was a party."

"Peter is treating us all to lunch!" chimed out Charles. "He has the department credit card."

"In that case, put me down for a bottle of your best merlot, and we'll take it from there," said James as he eased himself into the corner chair between Arthur and C.J. He gave C.J. a wink.

"Isn't Lauren with you?" C.J. asked pointedly.

"She wasn't in her office. Isn't she here?"

"No. I wonder where she is."

"No loss," said Walter, sourly.

"Why do you say that?" asked James.

Walter's answer was delayed by the arrival of more drinks. Glasses, bottles, and tumblers were distributed in front of everyone except for Betsy, who resolutely stuck to her water.

"Cheers," said Peter, raising his glass of red wine. "To a great semester. And a great department."

There was a murmuring of cheers and clinking of glass. Walter knocked back his scotch quickly, and waived the empty tumbler at Timothy.

Arthur drained his glass and felt his mood brighten. He hated office politics, but he loved office drama. This lunch had the potential to be very entertaining.

"Walter," Arthur said, poking the beast, "what were you saying about Lauren?"

"I was saying it would be no loss if she disappeared forever," Walter said. "She's not Eaton material, and I can't understand why she was hired at all. She's just sucking up valuable oxygen. That one's got to go, and the sooner the better."

"No need to hold back, Walter," said James, dryly. "Tell us how you really feel."

C.J. raised her eyebrows at Betsy. *The defensive lover, perhaps?*

"Is that your campaign position?" asked Peter, pouring himself another generous glass of cabernet sauvignon. "As chair, you'll start the semester by firing Lauren?"

Walter glared at Peter. "Not just Lauren. If I had my way, I'd get rid of all the incompetent faculty." Walter looked across at C.J., meaningfully.

"Oh, Walter," said C.J. "Me? Really? Stop it. You're too kind."

Walter ignored C.J. "Sadly, however, that power is not vested solely in the chair. At least, not currently. But what's your position, Peter? You hired the twerp. I assume you think Lauren Masters is an asset to the department."

"Well…" Peter stumbled for words. "Her potential is…"

"…as small as ant's patootie," finished C.J. "Come on, as much as it pains me to say it, Walter has a point. Who thinks Lauren Masters is going to get tenure? Anyone?" C.J. looked around the table. No one offered a defense of their colleague. "I didn't think so. Wouldn't it be kinder to send her on her way now, instead of having her fritter away five years and then cut her loose? She can't even turn up to a lunch that she invited me to. The girl's a disaster."

Charles cleared his throat. "Well, now, I don't know. Remember, a weed is a plant we've found no use for yet. As the vice chair candidate, I wouldn't want to dismiss Lauren like that. She's sweet, and with mentoring she could be something."

"I agree with Charles," said James. "Lauren's not a lost cause."

"Perhaps Walter here should take her on as his vice chair," suggested Charles. "If they lose the election, he could mentor her anyhow for the next few years. She isn't half-bad to look at Walter. It could be worse."

C.J. looked at Charles. "Vice chair? What are you talking about, Charles?"

"I'm running as Peter's vice chair. To give his ticket the voice of experience."

Peter cleared his throat. "It's not an official position, of course. The election is only for chair. But yes. If I were chair, Charles would be in a position to share his wisdom."

"Like no teaching for faculty older than seventy," said Charles.

"Who would teach your classes?" asked James. "Not me, that's for sure."

"It would be an opportunity for the junior faculty to develop their teaching skills," said Peter. "So perhaps we should hold off on firing them, Walter."

"Don't lie," said Walter. "If you relieve the geriatrics of their teaching, everyone else is going to have to teach more." Walter looked across at James. "I realize the importance of your research time. I would never impose a heavier teaching burden on you."

"Can the vice chair vote in the election?" asked C.J.

"No!" exploded Walter.

"Of course!" said Peter. "It's merely an endorsement of the chair candidate."

"I was just thinking about the quorum," said C.J. "We need five people to vote in the election."

"What happens if the quorum isn't reached?" asked Betsy.

"The election is postponed to the start of next semester," explained Peter.

"Wouldn't that be good for you?" asked Betsy. "You could continue on as acting chair."

"Well, I'd prefer to win today and hold the position for the next three years," countered Peter.

"You're not going to win," said Walter. "And you can't delay the election. The quorum is five. We have at least five people able to vote today."

"Unless we don't let the vice chairs vote," offered C.J. "Are you sure you want to deny Charles his vote, Walter?"

Walter did some quick math. He knew Charles would vote against him, but he wasn't sure that quorum could be reached without him. "We can discuss it when we meet to vote," he hedged.

"I didn't realize how powerful my vote was," said Arthur, thoughtfully. "Do you mean to say that if I don't turn up for the election, Peter is automatically reappointed chair for the next six months?"

"If your absence means we fall below quorum," said C.J., "then yes. Are you considering not voting?"

Arthur looked at the two candidates. "I'll vote if it's worth my while."

James turned to Walter. "Are you considering Charles's suggestion? Have you talked to Lauren about being your vice chair?"

"I don't need a vice chair. And, even if I wanted one, there's no way in hell I'd consider that walking Barbie as my vice chair. A woman's place is in the secretarial pool, not taking up precious office space."

At Walter's comment, Betsy looked up from her iPad, where she'd been trying to post on Facebook that she was out to lunch at Antonio's. Betsy looked from Walter to C.J and back again. She wasn't sure both of them were going to leave the restaurant alive. Should she post the impending death of a faculty member on Facebook?

C.J. turned an icy gaze on Walter. "Tell me, Walter," she said coolly, "will it be your official department chair policy to sort the staff by body parts? Ovaries to the secretarial pool, testes to the faculty lounge, jack asses to the chair's office?"

Timothy, misinterpreting the silence at the table as a good moment to take orders, approached with a smile. "Ready to order lunch?"

12:53 p.m.

Forty minutes later—a time during which several bottles of wine and close to fifty thousand calories of food had been consumed—the tension at the economics lunch table had completely dissipated. Snarky conversation had been replaced by chewing, slurping, and the clink of cutlery. Electoral ambition was muted by wine. And professional judgments were suspended, albeit it briefly, while the faculty digested their food.

James Brimmage pushed back his chair, sighing with satisfaction. The white tablecloth in front of him was stained with rare steak juice, pasta sauce, and red wine. He knew the empty wine glasses and half-drunk coffee on the table indicated that it was time to think about returning to the office. His one o'clock work hour was approaching. "I love being an economics professor," he confessed. "I bet only the law nerds and business school jerks have as large an expense account."

Walter, with alcohol-induced friendliness, smiled. "Imagine being a political science professor. I hear they only eat well every four years. Or a member of the Philosophy Department. They debate the ethical merits of ordering lunch until it's time for dinner."

C.J. snorted a laugh, which caused more giggles to break out around the table. Everyone at lunch understood the universal truth—economists were superior to everyone else. Even the most incompetent economist was more gifted, more handsome, and more talented than the most capable lawyer, political scientist, or philosophy major. That was why there was a Nobel Prize for economics, and no other social science.

Peter picked up the theme. "A sociologist, a philosopher, and an economist walk into a bar. The economist buys them all a round because the other two are unemployed."

C.J. snorted again, and more alcohol-infused snickers followed. Nothing united a group of people more quickly than a mutual dislike of someone else. Even Arthur laughed. As a rule, he disliked juvenile humor. But sometimes, when the moment was right, it amused him. "I wouldn't be so quick to judge the other professions. After all, an economist is someone who gets rich explaining to others why they're poor."

"Or someone who knows the price of everything and the value of nothing," quipped C.J.

Betsy, who was completely sober, was far too shy to start yelling jokes across the table. However, she loved a good economics joke as much as the next person. So she typed, "Economics has gotten so rigorous we've all got rigor mortis," on her Facebook wall. *I wonder how many* likes *that will get?* she thought as she posted it.

Charles, who'd appeared to be sleeping, opened his eyes and coughed. "Ahem. Now, it isn't true that economists are all useless. There was a woman I knew who heard from her doctor that she only had a half a year to live. Cancer, I think it was. The doctor advised her to marry an economist. The woman asked, 'Will this cure my illness?' The doctor replied, 'No, but the half year will seem pretty long.'"

Peter banged his spoon on the table to quieten down the laughter and get the attention of the crowd. "We all know the true state of affairs. On the first day God created the sun, so the Devil countered and created sunburn. On the second day God created sex. In response the Devil created marriage. On the third day God created an economist. This was a tough one for the Devil, but after a lot of thought he created a second economist."

Timothy, who'd been delighted by the amount of alcohol consumed, approached the table. "It looks like everyone is having a good time. Is there anything else I can get for you? Some more dessert, perhaps? Or another bottle of wine?"

"Nothing more for me," said James. "I need to get back to the office."

"I need to get moving as well," said Betsy. "I'm teaching at one."

Arthur scrunched his face in disgust. He hated even the mention of students.

"What a bunch of lightweights," said Walter. He turned to Timothy. "I guess you can get the bill. But make sure you give it to him." Walter pointed at Peter.

Peter held out a credit card to Timothy. "I trust your addition. Just run the card."

"That's not very fiscally responsible," mocked Walter, as Timothy left with the bill. "Are you going to let him decide his own tip as well?"

"Of course not. I'll tip the usual fifteen percent."

"Fifteen?" asked James. "I thought twenty was the norm these days."

"I never tip," said Walter. "What's the point? We've already received the service. When I'm reinstated as department chair, I won't waste money on tips."

Betsy looked at her watch. It was getting close to one o'clock. She needed to get to her class and was happy for the excuse to leave. It sounded as if the conviviality of lunch was wearing off, and she didn't want to listen to any more bickering.

"If you'll excuse me, I need to get going. Thanks for

lunch, Peter, It was delicious."

C.J. waved her friend goodbye and turned back to Walter. "Seriously? You don't tip at all?"

"Never. It doesn't make economic sense."

"What about as an incentive for good service?" asked C.J.

"That only makes sense if you're going to see the person again. Have you ever had the same taxi driver twice?"

"I think Walter has a point," said James. "Are we ever going to be served by our waiter again?"

Hopefully not all together, thought C.J. *I'm beginning to remember why I hate group lunches. The company sucks.*

Timothy returned with the bill and placed it in front of Peter, smiling. He was confident that his tip would exceed twenty-five percent. Timothy withdrew politely and everyone at the table looked at Peter expectantly.

"What?" he asked.

"We want to know how much you're going to tip," said C.J.

Peter, sensing that the tip issue had become something bigger, more of a statement about his chairmanship than a reflection of quality service, paused. "Let's decide as a table," he said.

"No tip," said Walter.

"I agree," said James.

"Five percent," said C.J. "A tip is supposed to be a reflection of the service. Timmy was annoying and arrogant before you gentlemen arrived."

"I'd leave twenty," said Charles. "The young man was very nice."

Peter looked over to Arthur. "Arthur?" he asked. "How much would you leave?"

"I don't care as it's not my money," said Arthur.

"I see," said Peter, doing the arithmetic. "Including

my fifteen, the average of our tips is eight percent. That's what I'll tip." Peter filled out the receipt and signed it.

"How very methodical of you," said Charles. "I guess we can't argue with the data."

"I don't know," said James. He was slowly sobering up from lunch and feeling a little punchy. "Do we really think Peter's analysis is that reliable? He just ignored Arthur's non-response."

"What do you mean?" asked Peter, bristling visibly. Any remnant of goodwill at the table was quickly evaporating.

James, who'd only intended his comment as a joke, floundered for a response to Peter's obvious anger. "Mate, you know what I mean," he said lamely.

"I don't think we do," observed Arthur.

C.J. wondered how much James had had to drink. He wasn't making any sense. But, more importantly, she was concerned that he'd warmed to Walter over lunch. *Had they really agreed on never tipping?* If James voted for Walter that afternoon... It didn't bear thinking about. C.J. looked at her watch. It was almost one o'clock. If she was going to influence the election outcome, it had to be now.

"Ya' know," C.J. began, with the exaggerated Texan twang, "one of my all-time favorite economic theories is the stated preferences versus revealed preferences."

"How interesting," said Walter, pushing his chair back. "But I need to get back to the office."

C.J. ignored Walter. "The classic case is when you ask people if they'll pay extra for shade-grown, happy-bean, sun-warmed-water coffee, and they say 'of course.' They *state* a preference for this amazing coffee. But put them in the store where the happy-bean coffee is a dollar more and they won't pay. They *reveal* in their actions they don't care a horse's patootie for the bean's happiness." C.J. took a sip of her own coffee and made a face. It was cold. "Which makes me think of you, Peter."

Peter, who'd been gathering his coat and hat in readiness to leave, looked up at his name. "Me? What about me?"

"For the last few months, you've stated that you took the acting chair position just for the good of the department. That you didn't really care about holding a position of power. But now it's election day, I see you are doing some serious campaigning. You have a vice chair, for no other reason than to secure votes—sorry, Charles. And you've paid for this expensive lunch. So your actions reveal that you really want to be chair. Am I right?"

Walter stopped, hands resting on the back of his leather dining chair, and waited to hear Peter's answer.

"Well, if it was good for the department..." Peter began.

"Phooey," said C.J. "What I like about Walter here, and, let's be clear, there's very little I like about Walter, is that he leaves us in little doubt about what he wants. He wants the chairmanship. Do you?"

"Well, yes," admitted Peter.

"Very good," said C.J. "Then it seems you've got an hour to win this thing. Arthur, James, and Lauren should be your campaign targets. The rest of us have known you so long, there isn't anything you could say that would change our minds."

"I tried to meet with Lauren," defended Peter. "But she didn't show up."

"So try again," said C.J. "I don't know where the woman is, but if you want to be chair you should find her."

"Perhaps she's wrapped up in some research," offered Charles.

"Charles, really. Remember, Occam's razor. The simplest, most reasonable explanation is most likely to be correct," C.J. chided. "Lauren doing research is so far-fetched. There's a greater chance the woman is dead."

C.J. turned to Arthur and James. "You have one hour to make up your minds about our two esteemed candidates. Neither one is grade A beef. But, for what it's worth, I think Peter has done a decent job for the last few months."

Walter, unable to contain his anger any longer, leaned over the table and banged his fist down hard. The coffee cups rattled in their saucers, and one wine glass fell to the ground with a smash. "You can't do this. I'm going to be chair. The job is mine. I deserve it. I'll hunt down anyone who thinks they can get between me and the chairmanship."

C.J. leaned back in her chair, satisfied. She'd been waiting all lunch for Walter to get liquored up and lose his temper in front of James and Arthur, the two swing votes. As her daddy always said, sometimes when you are a-hunting, you have to sit in the blind and wait for the game to come to you.

ONE O'CLOCK

1:04 p.m.

Mary Beth Sanders sat in her swivel chair, glaring out her office window. She watched various faculty members from the Economics Department weave their way up Knollwood Place. *Another liquid lunch that I have to file the paperwork for*, she thought resentfully. The receipts for these *working* lunches always ended up on Mary Beth's desk, and she was amazed each time. The professors ate steak and lobster. They drank wine by the case. They always ordered dessert. The totals were inevitably hundreds and hundreds of dollars. Enough for a complete day-spa, plus new shoes.

Life really wasn't fair. She'd spent her lunch hour at Bruegger's Bagels, eating a plain bagel with low-fat cream cheese. The bagel had been quite tasty, and she'd enjoyed reading her favorite magazines. However, everything is relative. And a bagel you pay for yourself is nowhere near as satisfying as a one hundred dollar, merlot-soaked lunch at Antonio's, paid for by the college.

Just wait until I'm a professor's wife, and you have to invite me too, she thought. Mary Beth frequently fantasized about going to these lunches. She was always wearing a mink coat, loads of diamond jewelry—though sometimes she thought she'd wear pearls as they seemed more classy—and the professors swooned over her, opening doors and attending to her every need. It was always the biggest jerks, like Walter

Scovill, who did the most sucking up. They asked her advice on shopping, listened to her views on the latest fashion trends, and laughed at all her jokes. Recently, Mary Beth's imagined lunch included a scene where she *accidently* spilled red wine all over Lauren Masters, causing Lauren to run away in tears and never return to the department again. Mary Beth loved the lunch-as-a-faculty-wife fantasy. She just needed a husband to make it happen.

As James Brimmage hadn't yet proposed, Mary Beth looked over at the work she needed to do with distaste. On the top of the pile of photocopying was Lauren Masters' syllabus marked *urgent*. *Yeah, well, I, like, urgently need to be taken out to a fancy lunch,* thought Mary Beth cattily. Looking back out the window, Mary Beth noticed Arthur Fleitman wending his way up the street with Charles Covington, and cut her eyes at him. *He's late for sensitivity training,* she thought.

Mary Beth strummed her perfectly manicured nails on her desk, trying to decide how to occupy her afternoon hours. She probably should make sure the new professors went to their training before that nasty lady from human services called again. Of course, there was always photocopying and filing. And Mary Beth had a vague recollection that she was supposed to type some letters. *But some days,* Mary Beth told herself, *a girl just needs to take a break from the whole work thing. Otherwise, you know, the risk of burnout was just too high.* Mary Beth flung her faux-cheetah-fur boots up onto her desk and loaded up another episode of *Say Yes to the Dress* on Netflix.

1:07 p.m.

There was no other way to say it. Charles Covington III and Arthur Fleitman were both very drunk. Charles had, of course, preloaded before lunchtime. And Arthur had caught up with him, sucking down the red wine like a thirsty man reaching an oasis. The overall effect on both men was similar, however. They were uncharacteristically upbeat.

"I need to unwind," Charles told Arthur as they stumbled up Knollwood Place together. Charles made a drinking motion with one hand, to translate what he meant by *unwind*.

"I'm supposed to be at sensitivity training," confessed Arthur.

"What the heck is that?"

"I don't really know," said Arthur, beginning to giggle. "And I guess I'll never know, as I'm not going."

"Good for you," said Charles. "Who needs sensitivity?"

The two men continued along Knollwood Place. Charles broke the silence after a few moments.

"I need to unwind," he said again. "You know what I mean?"

"Sure do. I'm working much too hard myself," agreed Arthur. "Did I tell you I'm supposed to be at sensitivity training?"

"Really?"

"Yep, but I'm not going. I'm too busy."

"Same here," said Charles. "I've been so busy that I haven't had time to think about my lecture for tomorrow."

"You teach history," said Arthur. "Surely it hasn't changed since last year. Just reuse your notes."

"I still have to find them before tomorrow."

"I hate students," observed Arthur conversationally.

"We all do," said Charles. "They're annoying."

"Did you know," asked Arthur, "that annoying people have been knocking on my door all morning? It made it hard to sleep."

Charles shook his head and tutted with sympathy. Neither man seemed to remember that Charles had been one of those annoying people.

"Do you know" asked Charles, "that my wife makes me go to couples therapy every week? I don't know who's more annoying. Her or the therapist. They're always telling me to *seize the day* and *make my own happiness.*"

Arthur patted Charles on the arm. Even in his intoxicated state, he knew he hated marriage. He pitied all men who were foolish enough to be roped into it. "You know, Charles, maybe that's good advice."

"Whadaya mean?"

"You and I. We should make some happiness. How long do we have until that stupid vote?"

"An hour, give or take. Long enough to grab a drink," suggested Charles hopefully.

"We can do better than that. I say we seize the heck out of this day. And your wife can't object. It was her advice."

"Seize how?"

Arthur started giggling. "Where's the nearest club?"

"Club? What type of club?"

"A strip club, you fool. We deserve some Mata Hari."

Charles snickered. "It's only one o'clock in the afternoon."

"All the better. It'll be less crowded. You got a better idea?"

Charles looked thoughtful, and then started snickering again. "Think we can charge it to the departmental expense account?"

"It's a research expense," snorted Arthur.

"Yeah. We're studying a stripped-down economic model," said Charles.

"Or top-down economics." The two men clutched at each other to prevent themselves from falling over from laughing.

"Or..." Charles couldn't get the words out he was laughing so hard. "Or...bottoms up!"

Arthur wiped tears from his eyes. "Now, seriously," he said, putting a hand on Charles's shoulder, "do you know if there's somewhere close by?"

"Of course," said Charles.

1:13 p.m.

Walter Scovill sat in his office and carefully lined up an after-lunch pick-me-up on his desk. A snort of happiness, as it were. A snuffle of sunshine. He took a bill from his wallet—he had no idea of the denomination—and vacuumed the cocaine up his nose. *Much better,* he thought, as the powerful drug began to fade the memories of the miserable lunch. Walter had no respect for any of his colleagues and considered time spent with them to be time wasted.

He leaned back in his desk chair and closed his eyes. Oh, there were so many wonderful things he was going to do when he was chair again. Like ridding the department of C.J. Whitmore. And Peter, for that matter. *Hell, why stop there? They could all go.* Excited by this idea, Walter opened up C.J.'s email about Betsy Williams and the teaching award. His first reply had been too nice.

TO: Tenured Faculty
FROM: Walter Scovill
SUBJECT: RE: Betsy Williams Teaching Award
Betsy Williams, and anyone who supports her teaching award, should leave Eaton and teach at Harvard. It will definitely raise the IQ around here and—given the disgraceful state of the economics profession—will probably do the same at Harvard.
W.S.

Walter felt a rush of adrenalin as he pressed send, but sighed afterwards. One email wouldn't do it. Until he managed to become malevolent dictator of the Economics Department, he needed to win today's election. His aspirations to clean up the department would amount to nothing if Peter Johansson was in charge.

Walter looked at the two lists written on his whiteboard. Could he count on the votes of James, Arthur, and Charles? James, of all the lunch companions, had seemed the least inane. He had, at a minimum, recognized the futility of the tipping system. James clearly appreciated the value of money. Perhaps Walter could secure his vote with an appropriate incentive. *I'll promise him a research grant, conditional on me becoming chair,* thought Walter. *And with no expectations that he use it on research, of course.* Walter wondered how large a research grant would guarantee him James's vote. *Would $100,000 be enough? He'd make it $150,000, just to be sure.*

As for Charles Covington…vice chair indeed. Peter Johansson was going to pay dearly for that bit of political maneuvering. *And Arthur Fleitman?* Walter just shuddered. Everyone has a price. What did Arthur want in exchange for his vote? Surely, not a vice chair position. The man was only in his seventies. *I'd be stuck with him for decades.* Walter wished he knew some deep, dark secret of Arthur's, so he could blackmail the man for his vote instead.

Walter stood up and walked over to the whiteboard. He erased Charles's name from his side of the list and wrote it under Peter's column. Walter studied the two lists. In his column he had James and Arthur. In Peter's column was written C.J., Lauren, and now Charles. Clearly, he had to deal with Lauren in order to win the election.

I'll start with James, he thought. *He's young and attractive. I'll get him to ask Lauren Masters to vote for me. She'll be flattered.*

1:15 p.m.

"I thought I could count on your support, C.J." said Peter reproachfully.

C.J. and Peter were seated in the faculty lounge, drinking strong, black coffee. C.J. had made a fresh pot, hoping to counteract the effects of lunch.

"And you can," C.J. said. "Talking of support, did you mean what you said about Betsy's teaching award? I really want to nominate her."

"Of course I meant it. I wouldn't have said it otherwise." Peter gave C.J. a petulant look.

"Is this about what I said at lunch?" she asked.

"I wasn't expecting the surprise attack. That's for sure."

"But it worked," countered C.J.

"What do you mean, it worked?"

"Walter Scovill lost his cool and showed his true leadership style."

"I guess." Peter took a sip of coffee and checked his

iPhone for messages. He opened the email from Walter. "I guess, in Walter's opinion, Betsy shouldn't get the teaching award." Peter held out his phone to C.J. so she could read the email. She squinted at the tiny screen.

"I can't read something that small," she complained.

Peter took back the phone and enlarged the font. He handed it back to C.J. She raised her eyebrows as she read.

"Opinions are like rear ends," C.J. said bluntly. The black coffee had induced both sobriety and a headache. She didn't have the energy for politeness. "Some are just smellier and louder than others."

"I don't think your speech at lunch helped my chances in the election," said Peter, ignoring C.J.'s bad mood and returning to the issue of the election.

"Stop whining and look at the math," said C.J. "Judging by who's around campus today, I think we'll have five people show up for the vote this afternoon. Which is, by the way, the minimum number we need for a quorum. You know that, right?"

"Oh, sure. Five for a quorum."

"So, you need three votes. I'm one."

"Right."

"You secured Charles, by making him vice chair. That was very clever, by the way."

Peter nodded his head in acknowledgement.

"Do you know for certain that you have a third vote? I meant what I said at lunch. You need to be campaigning for the votes of Lauren, James, and Arthur."

"I tried to see Lauren today. She missed a coffee meeting with me."

"Don't feel special. She stood me up for lunch. I hope she shows up for the vote."

"Well, if she doesn't and we miss quorum, you get six more months of me as chair. That's not so bad, is it?"

"I thought you wanted to secure the permanent position."

"I do. And I think I will. James assured me I had his vote."

C.J. pursed her lips together. "You know, it's easy to promise a vote in a secret ballot. There's no way to prove you didn't do as you promised. If Walter offers James the vice chair, then you might lose both James' and Lauren's votes."

"Why are you pairing Lauren and James together?"

"I don't know. It's just a hunch. "

"Are they a couple?"

"I don't think they're going to get married, if that's what you're asking. But I have a hunch they are…close, if you know what I mean."

"Really?"

"Don't quote me on it. What about Arthur's vote?"

"He wanted to support Charles, so I guess I have it."

C.J. looked exasperated. "You guess? Arthur Fleitman is a curmudgeonly old fool. It wouldn't surprise me if he voted for no one, just to amuse himself. Finish up that coffee and get campaigning."

1:18 p.m.

Betsy stood in front of her class, sipping hesitantly at a peppermint tea. Betsy didn't usually drink tea, and she was uncertain if she liked the taste. It tasted like hot water, nothing more. She'd been tempted to buy it when she stopped in at Wallaby's on her way to class. Her iPad had mentioned that tea helped a person lose weight, fight cancer, and was a virtual cure for diabetes. After an overly rich lunch of veal scaloppini with saffron cream sauce (and a dessert of tiramisu), Betsy figured she needed all the help she could get.

She smiled up at her class, who were filling out their get-to-know-you surveys. They were very quiet, and Betsy interpreted that to mean they needed a few more minutes to complete the task. Of course, she realized it could also mean they were texting, but she preferred to give them the benefit of the doubt. Bored, and wanting to pass the time, Betsy Googled "peppermint tea calories." She clicked on the first link and smiled. No calories. She took another sip and made a face. It appeared calories were positively correlated with taste.

Still wanting to wait another minute before starting the class discussion on the definition of economics, Betsy clicked on her Facebook app. Nothing new from the elusive Lauren. Her grandchildren were also silent—a good thing too, as they were supposed to be in school. A friend from church had posted a link to a new hamburger casserole recipe.

Facebook, sensing her need to procrastinate, informed her that a politician and his sex scandal were trending news. Betsy just shook her head. She didn't understand such people. And, still wanting to be helpful, Facebook suggested Betsy might like to make friends with the friends of her friends. The list, titled PEOPLE YOU MAY KNOW, was predominantly a collection of teenagers and tweenagers. Apparently one grandchild or another was a mutual friend. Betsy thought Facebook might want to review their algorithm, as she didn't want to know other people's grandchildren, just her own.

However, the last name on the list caught her attention, as it was a work colleague. "Lauren Masters is a mutual friend," Facebook informed her. Betsy wondered about the reliability of Facebook. She wouldn't have picked those two to be friends, online or in person. Betsy clicked open her email and sent a message to C.J., with the subject line "I don't like to gossip, but…"

1:25 p.m.

"What do I look like? Your goddamn secretary?" Mary Beth snapped at Peter in frustration.

Peter hated to point out the obvious, but Mary Beth did look like his secretary. Because that was what she was. Secretary, administrative assistant, whatever she wanted to call herself. She was there to do the paperwork.

"Um," Peter hesitated. "I guess…a little." Peter still held the offending receipt from lunch in his hand. "So, if you don't mind, could you please file this expense for me?" He placed it gently on her desk and started to back out of the office.

"Oh, sure," Mary Beth muttered to the retreating professor. "Don't mind me. I don't have anything better to do."

Mary Beth looked at her computer screen, which was filled with the freeze frame of a plump woman swaddled in a princess style wedding dress. *No offense, but it makes you look even fatter than you are,* Mary Beth said silently to the bride-to-be. *And I didn't think that was possible.* She angrily closed Netflix and stared at the receipt from Antonio's. *Nine hundred fifty-eight dollars? For lunch?*

At that moment, the phone on Mary Beth's desk rang. "Eaton Department of Economics," she said in her singsong phone voice. Mary Beth prided herself on her professionalism. It was important to be nice on the phone. There was always the possibility that an eligible bachelor was calling. "This is Mary Beth speaking."

On the other end of the line was the woman from human resources. The woman from human resources didn't waste any time before starting in with her complaints. Mary Beth lost the facade of pleasantness.

"Hey, lady," interrupted Mary Beth. "It's not my fault if none of them showed up to your training."

The woman continued.

"Of course I told them about the training," replied Mary Beth, conveniently forgetting that she'd never spoken to Lauren Masters. "But they're, like, professors, you know? Smart, but useless. They probably got lost on the way over."

Mary Beth hung up the phone without bothering to say goodbye. *Whoops,* she thought sarcastically. *It seems we got disconnected.*

Mary Beth then *filed* the Antonio's receipt by placing it on top of Lauren Masters' photocopying, stood up, fluffed her hair, and pushed up her breasts. She was, like, totally done with assisting. And she wasn't going to just sit back and watch Netflix for the rest of the day, either. It was time for action. If Mary Beth wanted to achieve her life's goals, she had to go out and get them. It was time she landed Mr. Rich Husband.

Mary Beth walked out of her office and down through the Smythe Lounge as quickly as the heels on her faux-fur boots would allow. As she crossed the lounge towards 42 Knollwood, she saw C.J. Whitmore coming the other way.

Mary Beth nodded at C.J. Thankfully, that woman was no threat to her plans. Someone as good-looking as James Brimmage was never going to be attracted to someone like that. C.J. Whitmore was an embarrassment to their gender. Who wore hot pink cowboy boots? And her hair! It was a frizzy, blonde, flyaway mess. Mary Beth would be willing to bet that C.J. didn't even own a straightening iron.

"Where's the fire?" asked C.J.

Mary Beth looked at her blankly. "Fire? What fire?"

"It's an expression," C.J. explained. "You look like you're in a hurry."

"Oh," Mary Beth replied. *What did that have to do with a fire?* "No. I'm just going to see Professor Brimmage. He's late for some training. I need to remind him to go."

C.J. tried not to roll her eyes. Mary Beth was so transparent. It was a shame that she'd chosen a completely unsuitable target. Mary Beth had more chance of getting Arthur Fleitman to propose than she did James Brimmage. C.J. knew that the right thing to do would be to talk to Mary Beth. She could explain that James wouldn't make a good husband, and Mary Beth was a valuable, important person regardless of whether she was married or not. But that would take so much effort, and C.J. was still feeling the effects of lunch.

"Don't let me keep you," C.J. said, standing to one side. "Good luck!"

1:34 p.m.

The first thing I'll do when I'm elected chair, thought Peter, *is get rid of Mary Beth.* Maybe he could off-load her on the Forestry school. They were so nice over there that they were sure to take her. *Of course,* thought Peter, *we'd need to get a replacement. And for some reason, the college secretaries don't like working in the Economics Department.*

Peter scowled. *That's the big problem with women,*

he thought. *They're too demanding.* The truth was that Peter Johansson quite liked women. However, not that many women noticed Peter. He had had only a few girlfriends over the years, and he had no wife.

Peter, standing in front of Arthur's closed office door, ran a stressed hand over his bald head. He realized, thinking back over the day, that Arthur had never actually said who he was going to vote for. In the faculty lounge, before lunch, Arthur had mentioned that Peter had sewn up the elderly vote. But what if Arthur didn't consider himself elderly? *Perhaps C.J. was right. The man might not vote for anyone.*

Peter hesitated before knocking on Arthur's door. *Would it be so bad if Arthur didn't vote?* If the quorum wasn't reached, Peter would hold the chair position for another six months. And who was to say that quorum would be reached at the next election?

Of course, Peter reasoned with himself, *it would be better to secure the election now. Then he'd know he had three years in the position. And God only knew what bribes Walter had offered Arthur.* Peter knocked loudly on Arthur's door. *He would make sure Arthur understood that when Peter was chair, Arthur would be excused from all teaching.* Peter didn't hear a reply and knocked again. Still nothing.

1:39 p.m.

Charles and Arthur were nestled in on the platinum side of the Elm Groove Gentleman's Club. They were relaxing in comfortable chairs pulled close to the catwalk that dominated the center of the room.

"This place isn't bad," said Arthur. In front of Arthur, an unclad woman did the splits up the length of a pole, her left foot pointing to the sky and her back arched so much her head met her right foot on the floor.

Charles nodded in agreement as he sipped on a happy hour gin and tonic. He appreciated the comfort of the padded chairs. He was too old to endure a hard seat.

"It's almost homey," said Arthur. "I think that last woman's necklace read *Perfect Mom.*"

Charles nodded again.

"The variety actually works in their favor. The chubby, older ones make the young girls look terrific. Everything's relative."

Charles took another swallow of his drink. Even with his hearing aids in, it was hard to follow Arthur's conversation. The music was very loud. Besides, he was enjoying himself too much to chatter. Mildred was a wonderful wife, but she certainly wasn't as flexible as these girls. And these girls didn't talk nearly as much as his newly-emancipated wife.

"You know," Arthur continued, "I used to date the strippers back in New Jersey. One was even a student of mine. Earning her way through college."

Charles looked over in surprise. He must have misheard Arthur. "You've dated strippers?"

Arthur nodded. "Of course, the market system really works. You get what you pay for."

The two men lapsed into silence, watching the show in front of them.

"I can understand why you haven't retired," Arthur commented to Charles. "Hard to let go of the salary, especially when this is how you pass the day."

"I don't come here every day," Charles defended himself.

"Why not?" challenged Arthur. "Now I know about it, this will be my regular lunch spot. Much more satisfying than Antonio's."

Charles smiled vaguely, and wondered if he could ask the manager to turn the music down. He hadn't been able to decipher Arthur's last comment over the noise.

"You dog," said Arthur, misinterpreting Charles's wordless smile as an admission of daily attendance.

Charles, his eyes still on the stage, leaned towards Arthur to better hear what he was saying.

"By the way," Arthur said, changing topics, "I stupidly agreed to do a seminar this semester. Do you think C.J.'d mind if I got someone to sub for me? Someone like James?"

"A seminar?" Charles asked. "Did C.J. rope you into that?"

"Yeah. And I hate presenting seminars."

"Well, don't ask me to sub. I haven't presented a seminar since I got tenure over fifty years ago."

Arthur put down his drink and turned away from the display of dexterity on the catwalk in front of him. "You haven't presented a seminar in fifty years?"

"At least."

"I underestimated you, Charles."

Charles looked at his watch reluctantly. "Guess we ought to head back soon. I shouldn't be late, seeing as how people are supposed to be voting for me."

"Do you think you and Peter are going to win?"

"I don't know. Walter Scovill is one determined jackass. There's no saying what he'd do to win an election."

1:47 p.m.

Mary Beth sat in the dark corner of the Smythe Lounge, avoiding her office. The Smythe Lounge was devoid of the usual clusters of graduate students, drinking free coffee and wrestling with problem sets. *They probably have the week off,* Mary Beth thought. *Because their professors wanted an extra week of vacation. Nice life, if you can get it.*

Mary Beth was grumpy with the world, grumpy with her job, and grumpy with James Brimmage, as he hadn't been in the office. If he wasn't in his office, and he and Lauren were both missing the training, could they be off somewhere together? Even a glance at her beautiful manicure failed to cheer her. She sipped her coffee slowly, willing the minutes to pass. Her university-mandated afternoon break was at two-thirty. She just needed to go unnoticed until then.

Mary Beth watched Walter enter the Smythe Lounge from the 42 Knollwood side. He seemed fidgety and on edge but didn't seem to notice Mary Beth. Walter stopped at the coffee pot and poured himself a large paper cup. He paced back and forth, drinking his coffee and muttering to himself.

Idiots...I'll get rid of the lot...James Brimmage is a dead man....Johansson's going to wish he never set foot on this campus...get rid of the lot...imbeciles...

Mary Beth could only hear snippets of the monologue, but it was enough to snap her out of self-pity mode. *James Brimmage is a dead man? Her James? Why did Walter want to harm James?*

Mary Beth sat quietly in her corner of the room, listening carefully as Walter continued his rant.

Not going to put up with this...time for action...they've all disposable goods...even Lauren...

Mary Beth wondered what Lauren had done to attract Walter's rage. *Probably just being herself,* she thought. Moments later, Mary Beth was distracted from her hate for Lauren when Peter Johansson walked into the Smythe Lounge, from the 40 Knollwood side.

"Hello, Walter," he said. It looked to Mary Beth like Peter was having to make an effort to be civil.

"Your office is on the other side of the street," commented Walter.

Peter forced a smile. "Just visiting some colleagues. I *am* the current chair of this department."

"Acting chair," corrected Walter. "And not for long. What, another twenty minutes maybe?"

Mary Beth listened closely to the exchange. This was as good as reality TV. There was always a cat fight when you watched *The Kardashians* or *Real Housewives.* She looked back over to Peter. Was Professor Johansson going to let Professor Scovill get away with that?

"Time will tell, I guess."

Mary Beth was disappointed. That was, like, such a lame comeback.

"You'll have to excuse me," continued Peter. "I have some other visits to make before two o'clock. It isn't wise to take an election win for granted."

"You should take your loss for granted," said Walter. "It's inevitable."

Peter, who'd been walking across the Smythe Lounge in the direction of 42 Knollwood, stopped and turned back to face Walter.

"My loss is inevitable?" asked Peter. "I don't think it's *my* loss we should be counting on."

Mary Beth gave Professor Johansson a silent cheer. *You got him!*

"Who do you think is going to vote for you?" sneered Walter. "Not Arthur Fleitman—that man hates the weak and powerless. And not James Brimmage— you heard him at lunch. He thinks you can't even run a simple regression. And if you're missing his vote, you're probably missing Lauren's. Who does that leave? C.J. and Charles? You might as well concede defeat now, before you embarrass yourself."

That is, like, so nasty, thought Mary Beth in delight.

1:52 p.m.

C.J. sat at her desk, sipping her third cup of black coffee since lunch. She usually avoided alcohol during work hours, but somehow the unpleasantness of the company and the dreariness of the weather had outweighed her professionalism.

There wasn't much time until she needed to head over to 40 Knollwood for the election. Not enough time to get started on any work. Out of habit, C.J. clicked open her email. She reread the email from Walter that Peter had showed her earlier. Unable to let this pass by uncommented, she pressed *reply all*.

> *TO: Tenured Faculty*
> *FROM: C.J. Whitmore*
> *SUBJECT: RE: RE: Betsy Williams Teaching Award*
> *It is nice that Walter and I can agree on some things. And it seems we both feel that the department would be improved if some of the current members left. I fear, however, we do not agree on who the departing faculty members should be.*
> *C.J.*

As C.J. pressed send, a message from Betsy Williams caught her attention. *Gossip?* thought C.J. as she opened the email with interest. She read Betsy's message. *Really? That's a surprise,* she thought.

1:55 p.m.

James Brimmage had returned directly to his office after lunch and immersed himself in the second work hour of his day. He blotted out thoughts of women, elections, office politics, and fast cars, and just focused on his research.

A quick learner, he'd locked his door this hour. He didn't want Mary Beth wandering in. Or C.J. Whitmore, trapping him into unwanted seminars. James was regretting agreeing to the seminar and wondered if he could get someone to do it for him. *Like Arthur*, he thought. *That man has plenty of spare time.*

A sharp knock sounded at his door, penetrating the inadequate defenses of his Bose noise-cancelling headphones. James sighed. This was at least the third time someone had tried to visit in the last hour. What could possibly be this urgent? Surely not the new faculty training. Hopefully, Lauren had gone, and James could get any necessary information from her. *It's probably about about the stupid election,* he thought. *C.J. sure riled up Walter and James at lunch.*

The person at the door knocked again. The knock sounded loud, insistent, and demanding.

James glanced at the clock on the computer monitor. It was almost two o'clock. "Just a minute!" he yelled out, as he removed his headphones, stood up, and walked over to unlock the door. Work was over for the day, and it didn't sound as if the person at his door was planning to leave him alone.

TWO O'CLOCK

2:02 p.m.

The conference room, where the election was being held, was located on the ground floor of 40 Knollwood, opposite Mary Beth's office. Arthur was the first faculty member to arrive. He'd come straight from the Elm Groove Gentleman's Club, and decided against stopping by his office before the meeting. He was tired from his afternoon activity, and the thought of climbing the stairs exhausted him.

Arthur hated meetings of any kind and despised elections in particular. Over the years, he'd adopted the policy of sitting in the back of the room, to minimize his expected role in the proceedings. The front seats were for the loud-mouthed agenda-pushers or the irritatingly eager. Arthur believed that meetings went against every economic principle he and his colleagues supposedly believed in. They were inefficient, they decreased productivity, and they wasted a person's most valuable resource—time.

He looked at the large clock on the wall. It was after two o'clock, and he was the only person in the room. Being kept waiting was another pet peeve for Arthur. He considered it rude, like walking around wearing ear buds, talking during a movie, and eating your food too quickly. *If no one shows up in the next five minutes, I'm out of here*, he promised himself. *It's not like I'm planning to vote for either Walter or Peter.*

2:06 p.m.

A few minutes later, Peter Johannson rushed into the conference room, his apologies tumbling out. "So sorry…delayed on chair business…unavoidable…came as soon as I could." He fell silent when he looked around and realized that Arthur was the only other person in the room. "Where *is* everyone?" Peter asked.

"Unavoidably delayed, I guess." said Arthur, who was annoyed at Peter for arriving just before he planned to leave. "Isn't that the excuse you just used?"

"Yes, well, I'm here now. We need the others. Where are they?"

"If no one turns up soon, I'm out of here."

"You can't leave. You said you'd support Charles, and Charles is on my ticket."

"Actually, I haven't promised my vote to anyone."

"Sure you have. Remember all that talk about Charles and me securing the…" Peter paused, searching for the right word, "the…mature voters? When I'm chair, I'll eradicate teaching obligations for the over-seventy. Isn't that what you and Charles want?"

"Of course. That's why Walter promised the same thing." Arthur leaned back in his chair and closed his eyes. He was now bored as well as tired. For the entertainment value alone, it was time to inflame the situation again. Arthur sat up and looked at Peter.

"Besides, I don't know if you should be rushing to have the election," said Arthur. "I'm not sure Charles is in your camp anymore. Are you sure you have the votes?"

"What do you mean? Why wouldn't Charles be supporting me? He's my vice chair."

"He *was* your vice chair," said Arthur darkly.

"Was?" fretted Peter. "Where *is* everyone? The election was clearly scheduled for today. At two."

Arthur, wearying of teasing Peter, just shook his head. "I don't understand why you want the position of chair. It's a lot of paperwork and hassle. But, seeing that you do, it's after two o'clock. You're here. Walter's not. And, most importantly, there's no quorum. I say the job is yours for the next six months. Congratulations."

2:12 p.m.

"Where is everybody?" Walter Scovill demanded angrily. He'd just entered the conference room, with Charles Covington III trailing behind him. Charles had stopped by his office to fill his coffee cup with an afternoon pick-me-up.

"A bit late, aren't you, Walter?" Peter challenged his opponent.

"Do you know where everyone else is?" Walter asked Arthur, ignoring Peter altogether.

"No..." Arthur started to reply. However, Peter began talking over the top of him.

"And Charles, what do you have to say? Arthur tells me you aren't going to be my vice chair anymore."

Charles, who'd been slinking towards one of the back seats, turned around.

"What's that?" he said.

"Don't pretend you didn't hear me," said Peter, now yelling loudly enough that the entire building could hear. He looked back to Walter. "What did you do? Buy his vote? Is being in power that important to you?"

"I'm not the one yelling," said Walter coldly. "However, we're all enjoying this fine example of your leadership. Panicked, angry, hostile. What every department needs."

Charles settled into the seat next to Arthur. "Where did Peter get the idea I wouldn't be vice chair?"

"No idea," said Arthur. "But I'm enjoying the show. It's almost as entertaining as the Elm Groove."

Charles sipped from his coffee cup and offered the mug to Arthur. Arthur took a long pull.

"Who do you think will throw the first punch?" asked Charles.

"I'll bet twenty on it being Peter," said Arthur.

"You're on," said Charles.

"You're questioning my leadership? Mine?" Peter was still yelling at Walter.

"It doesn't matter what I think," said Walter, pointedly speaking very softly. "It matters what the department thinks." Walter didn't quite know what had set Peter off, but he'd use this outburst to his advantage. "And we're still waiting on some faculty, so we can hold this election. We appear to be short of a quorum."

Peter inhaled deeply, trying to regain his composure.

"Should we put a time limit on the bet?" Charles asked Arthur. "Say, by the end of the voting?"

"Seems reasonable," said Arthur. He had to admit, he was enjoying his ringside seat.

"Why don't you try and calm yourself, Peter," said Walter, his tone saccharine and condescending. "I'm sorry that you can't handle stressful situations well. In the mean time, I'll go and find out where everyone else is. After all, someone has to take charge."

2:17 p.m.

Walter walked out of the conference room and crossed the hall to Mary Beth's office. There he found C.J. Whitmore perched on Mary Beth's desk, and Mary

Beth sitting in her desk chair. Mary Beth had been enjoying an episode of *Say Yes* until C.J. had walked in.

"Why aren't you in the conference room?" Walter demanded of C.J.

"Well, my father raised me to believe it was rude to interrupt a performance. Either you were seated before it started, or you waited outside until intermission. As I was running a few minutes late, I decided to wait it out here in Mary Beth's office until you and Peter paused for breath."

Walter just glared at C.J. There was nothing he liked about this woman. "Do either of you know where Lauren Masters and James Brimmage are?" Walter asked both women, ignoring C.J.'s explanation.

"Neither of them are here?" clarified C.J.

Walter shook his head at her. Women were incredibly stupid sometimes. "Yes," he said sarcastically. "They're both sitting in the conference room. I was just testing to see if you knew that."

"I'm, like, so confused," said Mary Beth. "Why are you looking for them if they're already here?"

Walter turned his gaze on Mary Beth. "Remind me again what the minimum IQ is for your job. Somewhere between earthworm and goldfish, perhaps?"

Mary Beth pouted. She hadn't understood what Walter had just said, but she knew from his tone it hadn't been nice. "If James is missing, it's because of you."

"What are you talking about?" asked Walter.

"I heard you—in the Smythe Lounge earlier. Muttering about disposable goods. I know what *disposable* means, you know. It's, like, garbage disposal."

C.J. spoke up, hoping to cut Walter off before he told Mary Beth what he really thought about her. "Now that I think about it, I don't know if anyone has seen

Lauren since this morning. She was supposed to meet Peter for coffee, and she shined on lunch with me. I'm beginning to feel a little uneasy about her."

"She didn't go to her training," piped up Mary Beth.

"What training?" asked C.J.

"Something about sensitivity. It was for the new faculty. It started at one o'clock."

"Is James Brimmage at that?" asked Walter. "Tell me where it is. I'll get him."

"He's not there," said Mary Beth.

"How do you know?" asked C.J.

"The human resources woman called, like, thirty minutes ago. She said that *none* of the economics professors had shown up. So I went looking for Professor Brimmage."

"That's right," said C.J., remembering her earlier encounter with Mary Beth. "Was he in his office when you went to find him?"

"No."

"Did you actually look inside his office?" demanded Walter.

"No, the door was locked."

Walter smirked. "So we've got two missing professors and a locked door?"

C.J. raised an expressive eyebrow. Mary Beth scowled.

"I don't give a flying…" Walter stopped himself and rephrased his thought. "I don't care if Lauren Masters missed lunch at Antonio's. I don't care that Lauren and James missed some stupid training. And I certainly don't care if the two of them are doing the dirty on his office floor. The only thing that matters is that Lauren and James are in the conference room in the next five minutes, so we can vote for chair. Without them, we can't make quorum."

"I'll go look for them," offered Mary Beth.

"Actually," C.J. cut in before Walter could begin another tirade on Mary Beth's lack of competency, "we really need you to make a pot of strong black coffee and take it into the conference room."

"Okay," Mary Beth agreed, and headed out the office and down the stairs to the Smythe Lounge to make coffee. It was still snowing out, and given the day she was having, she'd probably find Lauren and not James.

C.J. opened Mary Beth's desk drawer and pulled out the set of master keys.

"I'm going to see what the deal is," she told Walter. "Why don't you take your patootie back to the conference room and make nice with Peter? I'll be back as soon as I can."

2:24 p.m.

C.J. crossed Knollwood Place and headed to 43 Knollwood first. It was still snowing heavily, and she didn't have a coat. She had used the Smythe Lounge underpass to get from her office to the conference room and hadn't planned on venturing outside. She hurried along the street, rubbing her arms to keep warm.

Now that she thought more about it, Lauren's absence all day was disturbing. Had she become ill? Maybe some highly contagious stomach bug was going around, and James had developed it after lunch. Or, maybe, Lauren had slipped on the snow and ice. She was always in high heels. But that wouldn't explain where James was. Perhaps Walter was right, and they were enjoying the afternoon together. That was a natural consequence of two young, attractive people working side by side.

C.J. walked into 43 Knollwood, stomped the snow off her boots, and walked hastily up the hall to Lauren's office door. *She really needed to think about the location of her next sabbatical,* C.J. thought. *Somewhere warm. Florida, perhaps. Or back home in Texas.*

C.J. knocked loudly on the door. "Lauren?" she called out. "Are you in there?" She tried the handle, but the door was locked.

C.J. waited but couldn't hear anything. She knocked again. "Lauren? We're worried about you. I'm going to let myself in."

Again, C.J. paused and listened, but the building was eerily quiet. She pulled out the master key for Lauren's office and unlocked the office door. C.J. slowly opened the door. If Lauren and James were…together…she didn't want to see it. "Lauren?" she said. "It's C.J. I'm coming in." As C.J. opened the door fully and looked in the room, she stopped. The chill that C.J. felt had nothing to do with how cold she was from the snow. Lauren Masters' dead body was slumped across her desk. Her throat had been sliced.

C.J. gently walked across the room and checked for a pulse, but Lauren was cold. Her body had begun to stiffen with rigor mortis, and C.J. realized the young woman had probably been lying dead in her office since that morning. *Had she been the last person to see Lauren alive? Besides the killer, of course.*

C.J. retraced her steps to the hallway, pushed the lock in on the door, and closed it. She checked the handle to make sure it was locked. C.J. didn't like Lauren Masters, but the woman deserved some respect and privacy in death. And she didn't want anyone else to disturb the crime scene. *Did James Brimmage do this? Was this why he wasn't around? Or…*A worse thought gripped at C.J. *Was he dead too?*

C.J. ran back across Knollwood Place, this time not even noticing the cold. She entered 42 Knollwood and sprinted up the stairs to James's second floor office. She knocked loudly on the door. "James!" she yelled. "I'm coming in!" She fumbled with the master key, her shaking hands preventing her from slipping the key into the lock. She forced herself to take a deep breath and slow down. She finally got the door open and lunged into the room, tripping over something at her feet.

With horror, C.J. looked down and saw James Brimmage—lying on his back on the floor of his office. Just like Lauren, his throat had been cut. She knelt down by his side. He wasn't as cold as Lauren, but C.J. recognized the aura of death. It was the same lifeless look that animals got after slaughter. Thinking back to that, C.J. realized that there wasn't much blood spatter in either office. She would have expected more if the carotid artery had been slashed. This was the work of an amateur. Only the trachea had been cut, meaning Lauren and James had suffocated—slowly and painfully.

C.J. sat quietly on the floor of James's office, next to his body, and thought about what she knew. Lauren had died before James. They'd both died the same way. And the killer was probably in the conference room right now.

2:41 p.m.

C.J. walked slowly through the Smythe Lounge towards 40 Knollwood. The lounge smelled like fresh coffee, but neither the coffee pot nor Mary Beth were around. C.J. climbed the stairs to the ground floor of 40 Knollwood and stood in front of the conference room door.

"I'm going to leave," she heard Arthur say. "It's clear we aren't having the election today."

"You owe me twenty if you leave now," Charles said loudly.

"What are you talking about? We didn't bet on whether there would be an election. The wager was on who would throw the first punch."

"We had twenty on the election as well."

"Is this true? Did you bet on the fact there wouldn't be an election?" challenged Walter. "Do you know something that we don't know?"

Arthur dismissed Walter with a wave of his hand. "All I know is the college rule on tardiness. Wait fifteen minutes for a tenured professor, ten minutes for an assistant, and five for an adjunct instructor. James and Lauren combined only come to twenty-five minutes. I'm done waiting."

C.J. heard the scraping of a chair and knew she couldn't stall any longer. She entered the conference room. The coffee pot was sitting in the middle of the conference table, but no one was drinking any. It appeared Mary Beth had forgotten the cups, as there were none in sight.

"Did you find them?" asked Walter.

"Please, everyone, sit down," said C.J.

Arthur and Walter sat down reluctantly.

"No one is going anywhere," said C.J. "Lauren Masters and James Brimmage are both dead. Murdered in their offices."

"Again?" asked Charles in amazement, referring to the fact that the Eaton Economics Department had experienced the murder of two colleagues the semester before.

"Can we still have the election?" asked Walter.

"Who did it?" asked Arthur.

"Who indeed," said C.J. "When was the last time anyone saw Lauren or James today?"

"I saw Lauren this morning, on the way to work," said Charles. "But a few hours later, when I knocked on her door, she didn't answer. Mary Beth was looking for her too."

"Anyone else see Lauren?" asked C.J.

"We were supposed to meet for coffee," said Peter. "But she didn't show."

"Who cares?" asked Walter. "We need to hold the election."

C.J. cut her eyes at Walter. "Did you see Lauren today?" she asked him pointedly.

"Only when she arrived for work. Which was surprisingly early for her. Well before ten."

"I saw her about the same time," C.J. added. "I stopped by her office in the morning. What about James?" asked C.J. "Did anyone see him after lunch?"

Everyone in the room shook their head. No one had seen James since lunch.

"I knocked on his door, to talk about the election," said Peter. "But there was no reply."

"When was that?" asked C.J.

"After we talked in the faculty lounge. So, maybe, an hour ago?"

"Have you called the police?" asked Arthur.

"Not yet. I thought we might chat about it first. It would be good to solve this before the police arrive. You weren't here last semester," C.J. said to Arthur, "but the last time we were in this situation the police were inept and irritating. I don't think anyone here wants to live through that again."

"And you're less of an irritant?" said Walter sarcastically.

"You think you can work out who did it?" asked Peter.

"Not me alone," replied C.J., answering Peter's question and ignoring Walter's. "But together, why not? We're supposed to be smart people. The average IQ in this room is close to two hundred. We should be able to figure out something."

Walter made a face to indicate that he wouldn't rate the average IQ of the people in the room so highly. His, of course, was that of a genius. But the rest of them?

"What are you proposing we do?" asked Charles. He hoped C.J. wasn't going to insist that they all talk about their feelings. He didn't have strong feelings on the deaths of Lauren and James. He barely knew them.

"Well, the answer is always in the data," said C.J. "We just need to look for the simplest scenario that explains the most. You know, Occam's...razor." C.J. tripped over the word *razor* as she realized that both professors had died from having their throats cut. The coincidence made her shudder. She went to the blackboard at the front of the conference room and started a list, headed "Things to Explain." Underneath she wrote: Lauren's death; James's death.

"For example, Mary Beth could have killed them both," C.J. said. "She certainly didn't like Lauren. But that was because Lauren was a competitor in the affection for James. Not that Mary Beth was ever going to be successful with James. But Mary Beth didn't know that. So she had plenty of reasons for wanting to kill Lauren, but none to kill James. And the explanation needs to cover why both people were killed. See my point? Mary Beth is not a likely suspect."

C.J. went back to the blackboard and wrote down the names: Mary Beth; Walter; Peter; Arthur; Charles. After a moment's thought, she added her own name to the list. "Assuming the killer is someone from the department who's here today, these are the potential suspects." Then she ran a line through Mary Beth's name. "She seems unlikely."

"Why are you limiting the suspect list to those in the department today?" asked Peter. "Anyone could have done it. Maybe some Australian relative of James's. They're all former convicts, you know."

"We're looking for the simplest explanation, Peter. Let's start with the people who're actually here."

"You're missing your friend Betsy," said Walter. "As she was included in our faculty lunch at Antonio's, I think she should be included on our suspect list."

C.J. wrote Betsy's name on the board. "The simplest explanation for Lauren missing coffee with Peter and lunch with me is that she was killed in the morning." C.J. decided not to mention how cold and stiff Lauren's body had been, though she knew this was further evidence supporting a morning time of death. It was still too gruesome to dwell on. "And Betsy was teaching class all morning, so I doubt she's our killer." C.J. drew a line through Betsy's name. No one objected. Walter thought that Betsy, like Mary Beth, lacked the intelligence for the crime. But he didn't voice his opinion as it was a personal principle to avoid agreeing with C.J. whenever possible.

Charles nodded eagerly. "The law of parsimony," he said. "I like it. Try me next. Could I be the killer?"

"Well, what reason do you have for wanting both Lauren and James dead?"

Charles paused, looking thoughtful. "Well, Lauren pretended not to see me this morning. Made me feel old, and none-too-good about myself."

"Anything else?" asked C.J.

"This is stupid," said Walter. "Let's just have the election and let the police sort this out."

"Hold your horses, cowboy. There isn't going to be an election. We don't have the quorum," said C.J. "But try to be useful. Can you think of a reason why Charles would kill them both?"

"To stop me being elected, obviously. Why else would they be killed on election day? As you just pointed out, without them we don't have quorum."

"Interesting," said C.J. "You're right. There *is* probably something in the fact they both died today." She went back to the board, and added, "Why today?" to her list of things that needed explaining. She turned back and looked at Walter.

"But why would Charles kill them both? Killing one is enough to get rid of the quorum."

"Either way, doesn't that put Walter and myself in the clear?" asked Peter. "We wouldn't want either dead, as it ruins the election."

C.J. looked thoughtfully at the list on the board, but didn't draw a line through either man's name. "I'm not sure," she said slowly. "The lack of election means that you'll continue to be chair."

"True, but being acting chair isn't the same as being chair. I've been a lame duck acting chair for the last six months. I don't want to repeat it."

C.J. responded by crossing Peter's name off the list.

"What?" asked Walter. "You believe that crap? Peter wasn't going to win the election. Stopping the election was his only chance of keeping any power at all. The man was a disaster as chair. Look at the people he hired."

"What are you saying, Walter? I thought you'd be thrilled about the fact that I joined the faculty," said Arthur.

C.J. held up a hand. "By all means, let's consider the fact that James and Lauren were both hired while Peter was chair. They're also both dead."

"Maybe I'm next," said Arthur.

"I wouldn't joke," said C.J. She turned slowly and stared at Walter. "We all know you hated the hires that occurred in your absence. You're not the most subtle person, in case you didn't know. One theory is that you killed them off, like a lion clearing out the offspring of another male."

"That's crazy!" sputtered Walter. "You're crazy."

"Crazy or not, it's a simple explanation."

"That theory is crap. I wanted the election. I can't bear the thought of another six months of Peter's incompetence," said Walter. "And if I did want to thin the herd, as you imply, there's no reason for me to do it today. If I wanted to get rid of them, I would've done it weeks ago."

C.J. picked up the chalk and put a line through Walter's name. The annoying thing about being data-driven was that sometimes you had to admit your enemy was right.

"Are you sure they were murdered? James could have killed Lauren and then committed suicide out of remorse," offered Peter. "Or they both could have killed themselves. Or each other, for that matter."

C.J. added James and Lauren to the suspect list on the blackboard and then thought back to the crime scenes she'd uncovered. She couldn't imagine either victim cutting their own throats. She drew a line through each name.

"I don't want to get into details of the crime scenes, but I think the possibility of either person committing suicide is extremely remote."

"Well, I'm still in favor of the earlier theory," said Walter. "Charles did it. Lauren and James were both young. He was threatened by their youth."

"That's a good one," said Charles. "Except, I didn't actually do it, you know."

Walter just snorted. "Oh, sure. And would you admit to it if you had?"

"Why would Charles have done it today?" asked

Arthur. "He was Peter's vice chair. He wanted the election to happen. It's not in his interest to decimate the quorum."

"I thought you said Charles didn't want to run as my vice chair," said Peter.

"I was lying. So sue me."

C.J. nodded, and put a line through Charles's name.

"I have another one," said Walter, ignoring both Charles and Arthur as he continued to vent at C.J. "You did it. James Brimmage never looked twice at you, not with someone as beautiful as Lauren around. What a blow to your ego, that he didn't want you. I think you killed them out of jealousy."

"Could be," said C.J. "But if I wanted to date James, it doesn't make sense for me to kill him. It's not my style to have a relationship with a corpse." C.J. didn't bother to add that it wasn't her style to have a relationship with someone as superficial and fickle as James Brimmage. That was a discussion for another day. "And it doesn't explain why I would have killed them today. As you said about yourself, why wait until today, when I could have killed them over the Christmas break?" C.J. crossed off her own name. "Unless anyone has an objection?" she asked the room. No one said anything.

"Arthur? You're pretty quiet," said C.J. "I don't have a line through your name yet."

"Well, complete lack of interest is my defense. I was surprised that someone like Lauren Masters was hired here. She was well below my caliber. But so what? Neither she nor James were worthy of my notice. So I guess it'll have to be a pretty complicated theory to get around that problem."

C.J. looked at Arthur carefully. "That's a great point," she said. She ran a chalk line through his name.

"I'm glad you're impressed by my lack of concern,"

said Arthur.

"No, not that," said C.J. "The point that you didn't think Lauren was Eaton caliber. At lunch today, we all agreed on that. At the moment, we've come up with theories why each of us could have killed them, but dismissed them as unlikely." C.J. pointed to the board where every name was ruled out. "Clearly, we're missing part of the story. What if the fact that Lauren was underqualified for her job is the key to this?" She added "Lauren unsuitable hire" to the list of things to explain.

C.J. pointed to the list. "There has to be a simple explanation. Why were James and Lauren killed? Why were they killed today, election day? And why was someone like Lauren ever hired in the first place?"

A heavy silence filled the room.

"Okay. Let's just answer Arthur's question. Why was Lauren hired?" C.J. asked.

"Don't ask me," griped Walter. "I wasn't here. I would never have hired her. I'm still trying to undo the mistake of hiring you."

C.J. grinned at Walter. "Aren't you the last of the sweet talkers? Don't worry. I love you too, Walter."

"She wasn't so bad," said Charles. "I always got the feeling she was ambitious. She just didn't work as hard as most junior professors."

"Who hired her?" asked Arthur.

"He did," said Walter, pointing at Peter. "While he was acting chair."

"Just Peter? Wasn't she chosen by a hiring committee?" asked Arthur.

"You and James were," said C.J., "but not Lauren. Last semester, we had to hire several people quickly, so the administration gave the chair the power to appoint a junior professor. Only tenured faculty hires required the full scrutiny of a committee."

"Who were you choosing between?" Walter sneered at Peter. "Were the choices Lauren and, I don't know, a dead rat?"

"Given the circumstances, I don't think we should be making jokes about the dead, Walter," said C.J.

"Fine. But we all know that Peter shouldn't have made the appointment. He should have waited until a permanent chair was elected."

"See what I mean about the problem of being an acting chair?" asked Peter. "Every decision is questioned. As I've explained before, she was the most qualified candidate."

"Tell us, Peter," continued Walter. "Why'd you do it? Hoping to get some gratitude action? As if someone as good looking as Lauren would ever notice you."

"Walter, please," protested Peter, looking pained at the crude suggestion. "She was the best candidate for the job. That's it. I'd never met her before, and I didn't ever see her socially."

"But that's not strictly true, is it, Peter?" asked C.J. slowly.

A silence settled around the room.

"I know you and Lauren had a history, because Facebook told Betsy."

"Who's Facebook?" asked Charles.

"Not a who," corrected C.J. "A what. Facebook is a computer site. And it lets you know who your friends' friends are. In this case, Betsy was friends with Lauren, and Lauren was friends with Peter."

"Who cares?" asked Walter.

"You should," said C.J., whose keen intelligence was working quickly. "I believe the key to this entire mess is the fact that Peter hired Lauren. She clearly wasn't Eaton quality, but he hired her anyway. Why?"

"You and Lauren were a couple?" asked Walter, incredulously.

"No, of course not," said Peter, running his hand over his bald head nervously. "I barely knew the woman."

"Charles, I think you struck on the issue," said C.J. "Lauren Masters was ambitious, but she was never doing any work. So what's the simplest explanation for why she wasn't working hard to get tenure?"

"She didn't want it?" asked Charles.

"That seems unlikely," said C.J. "Who wouldn't want tenure?"

"She knew she'd get it," said Arthur thoughtfully.

"Exactly," said C.J. "She knew the same person who hired her would make sure she got tenure—Peter. The only question is why. I think Peter here is telling the truth when he said he wasn't in a relationship with her. But clearly she knew something. What did she know about you, Peter, so that she could have this much power over you?"

Peter resolutely remained silent.

"Blackmail is such an interesting crime," said Charles. "It's not a crime to tell the truth. And it's not a crime to ask for a job or money. But it becomes a crime when you combine them."

C.J. nodded. "But the big problem with blackmail is that it never ends, unless you confess the secret or..." C.J. looked over at Peter. "...or you kill the blackmailer."

Peter said nothing.

"I think Walter was right," continued C.J. "It's important that the crimes occurred today, election day. Lauren wasn't the only ambitious person. Peter, as much as you tried to hide it, I know you really wanted to win. You enjoyed the power of being chair."

Walter snorted at Peter, as if to say that he'd never stoop to underhanded tactics to win an election.

"I can guess at how this went," said C.J. "She

wanted something else and was going to let your secret spill before the election unless you complied. It must have seemed never-ending. Always having to give Lauren whatever wish she thought up next. What was it this time? A better office? Research money?"

"None of this is true," argued Peter. "I thought she was the best person for the job. She didn't blackmail me, and I certainly didn't cut her throat to rid myself of the problem."

"Her throat was cut?" asked Charles.

"Yes," said C.J. "But I hadn't mentioned that. It was so brutal and unpleasant. I didn't want to talk about it."

Walter laughed heartily. "Hmm, let's see," he said, his voice laden with sarcasm. "What's the simplest explanation for the fact that Peter knew how Lauren died? Channel your inner Occam's razor, everyone. Let's think," said Walter, feigning a thoughtful look. "Could it be that Peter is the killer?"

Peter ignored Walter and looked at C.J. "She wanted to be promoted to a tenured position right away. With the appropriate pay increase, of course," said Peter. "And she insisted I push it through by today, in case I lost the election. How could I? A department chair can't make tenure appointments without faculty approval."

The room was quiet. Peter Johansson was a murderer? Harmless, innocuous, unexceptional Peter?

"What did she know?" asked C.J. quietly. "What was worth all of this?"

Peter waved C.J. away. "It's…complicated."

"When did you meet her?"

"At a conference, a few years ago. I was presenting a paper. She was a graduate student. I suggested drinks one evening and we got to talking. She told me she was worried that her research wasn't good enough. She didn't think she'd ever publish anything in a major journal. I just wanted to make her feel better. And I'd had a few drinks. So I told her that my one major publication, the one that got me tenure at Eaton, was completely specious. At the time, there was all this pressure to publish. It was taking me forever to collect the data. So I just used a random number generator to create most of the data set. The results, of course, are meaningless."

The room collectively inhaled. It was fine for professors to drink heavily, sleep with students, and put no effort into teaching. But to falsify research? That was egregious.

"She knew it would end my career. So she held it over me, to advance hers."

"But the thing I don't understand is why kill James?" asked C.J.

"I wasn't sure he didn't know. You said yourself that they seemed to have something connecting them. What if she'd told him my secret? I couldn't take the chance."

C.J. went to the blackboard. She erased everyone's name except for Peter's. Next to his, she wrote the word "ambition."

"The problem with Occam's razor," said C.J., "is that the simplest explanation is not always very pleasant." She looked at Peter. "I thought you were different than Walter."

"He is," interjected Walter. "I haven't killed anyone."

"Not yet," muttered Arthur under his breath.

"So that's it?" asked Charles.

"I think so," said C.J. "Ambition is the simplest explanation—the one that explains every aspect of this crime. Lauren's ambition led to the blackmail. And Peter's ambition resulted in the deaths of James and Lauren."

EPILOGUE

On the second Monday of the spring semester, Betsy Williams sat in Wallaby's coffee shop at eleven in the morning, waiting for C.J. Whitmore. The snow from the previous week had turned gray and slushy, and today the campus had a dreary feel. Perhaps it was the weather. Or the fact that this was the first time that Betsy had walked around campus without having to avoid newspaper reporters and TV crews. They'd been annoying, but there was a flat feeling now that the Eaton Economics Department was out of the spotlight again.

Betsy no longer had her iPad to read while she waited for C.J. The previous Saturday night, Betsy had Googled *snoring* while lying in bed next to Mr. Williams. After diagnosing her husband with sleep apnea, she kept poking him all night to make sure he didn't die. The next morning, the iPad was gone.

So instead, she was reading the student newspaper, *The Pug Post*. On the front page was a picture of Adorable Don XIII. Betsy smiled at his cute face and thought again she might like to get a dog.

Unfortunately, the feature article underneath the picture wasn't as heartwarming. Unlike the mainstream media, the school newspaper was still running stories about the murders in the Economics Department as front page news. Today was a clever piece on the monetary value of human life. "How much do we need to pay these professors so they won't kill each other?" the student-reporter challenged. Betsy shook her head.

Did the student really think money could overcome ambition?

"Betsy!"

Betsy looked up to see C.J. waiting in line for her coffee. She smiled at her friend, and her outfit. *Only C.J. Whitmore could wear hot pink cowboy boots with turquoise jeans*, she thought fondly.

A few minutes later, C.J. joined Betsy at the table. "Aren't you a clever one?" C.J. asked Betsy.

"What are you talking about?" asked Betsy.

"You had the paper in front of you. I thought you knew," said C.J. She grabbed *The Pug* and flipped through to a small article located towards the back. "See?" she said, holding it up for Betsy to see.

The article listed the finalists for the campus-wide teaching award. They were listed alphabetically, and at the bottom of the list was the name "Elizabeth Williams."

"You didn't get an email letting you know?" asked C.J.

Betsy looked delighted. "Oh, my goodness!" she said. "Really? I had no idea."

C.J. thought it best not to mention that Betsy had only received the nomination after she and Charles had written letters of recommendation, and C.J. had bargained with Arthur to do the same. In exchange for the letter, Arthur had demanded he be released from his seminar obligation.

"You deserve it," said C.J.

"That's enough about that," said Betsy, feeling uncomfortable with the spotlight. "How are you? I still can't believe what happened last week."

"Well, I'll tell you what I can't believe. The department elected Walter as the new chair this morning."

"As acting chair?"

"No such luck. The dean insisted we hold a special election, even though it wasn't the first day of term. I think he was worried that none of the faculty would be alive in six months."

"And Walter got the job?"

"Well, he was the only who ran for the position. Charles didn't even turn up to vote. I heard that Mildred took him to a couples retreat over the weekend. I'm sure the poor man is still recovering."

"Did you actually vote for Walter?"

"Of course not. I cast a blank ballot. But someone must have voted for the man."

"I wonder who it was?"

"My guess is Arthur Fleitman. Doesn't he remind you of Walter, somehow?"

Betsy shook her head. "I don't know Arthur that well. What about replacement faculty?"

"It's a little hard. We're getting a reputation. I guess Walter will look into it now that he's officially chair. In the meantime, I'm going to teach James's class for the rest of the semester. I agreed to do it in exchange for a sabbatical next semester. I don't know whether to be delighted that Walter agreed to the trade despite his natural inclination to be disagreeable, or offended with how happy Walter looked at the idea of getting rid of me."

"You're going on sabbatical? Where?"

C.J. looked out the window. "Somewhere warm. And murder free."

THE END

ABOUT THE AUTHOR

 J. T. Toman lives in Boulder, Colorado. When she isn't writing, she spends her time hiking, biking, and coaxing her vegetable garden to grow. Her previous publications include "Punishingly Younger" (*Skirt!,* June 2009), "Yesterday" (*Every Day Fiction*, Sept 2015), and *Picking Lemons: A C.J. Whitmore Mystery* (Cozy Cat Press, 2013).

www.ingramcontent.com/pod-product-compliance
Lightning Source LLC
Chambersburg PA
CBHW020341260626
47156CB00004B/1639